T0146745

SUMMONS TO DANGER

B.J. closed her toolbox. The fine hair on her neck rose, and she stood there, gripping a metal chair frame. If she just turned around . . . but she couldn't because she knew the street was empty, that nobody was there . . .

She'd been working too hard. It was too hot. *Nothing was wrong.*

"Annie?"

No mistake this time. The ghostly whisper was inside her head, faint but clear. It didn't matter that her name was Bethany Jean, and she'd never been called Annie.

She had no doubt the voice was calling to her . . .

"Vivid and highly atmospheric."
—Patricia J. MacDonald

"This is truly a wonderful book and ought not to be missed."
—Charles L. Grant

SOMETHING'S CALLING ME HOME

Maxine O'Callaghan

POCKET BOOKS

New York   London   Toronto   Sydney   Tokyo   Singapore

This book is a work of fiction. Names, characters, places and incidents are either the product of the author's imagination or are used fictitiously. Any resemblance to actual events or locales or persons, living or dead, is entirely coincidental.

An *Original* Publication of POCKET BOOKS

POCKET BOOKS, a division of Simon & Schuster
1230 Avenue of the Americas, New York, NY 10020

ISBN: 978-1-5011-4573-5

First Pocket Books printing February 1991

10 9 8 7 6 5 4 3 2 1

POCKET and colophon are registered trademarks of
Simon & Schuster.

Printed in the U.S.A.

For my brother, John Parrish,
and his wife, Jan,
with much love

SOMETHING'S CALLING ME HOME

Prologue

He stood in the doorway, staring at the old lady on the bed. In the dim light he could see what the shrunken face would look like once the worms had picked it clean. The room already smelled of rotting flesh. How did the old bitch hang on?

She shifted and opened her eyes. "Verna? Is that you?"

"Verna's resting."

He had coaxed Verna into taking a sleeping pill. Not that she needed much coaxing, tired as she was.

"I want Verna." A feeble whisper. "I want my medicine."

He stepped over beside the bed and put his hand on her head. Her hair felt like the gauzy stuff they used to spread on Christmas trees. She tried to twist away.

"Verna," she croaked.

He pushed her down, thinking how easily he could snap her brittle neck. He couldn't afford to give in to the urge. He knew that. Still, it was nice to savor the thought for a minute before he picked up a pillow and pressed it over her face.

She pawed at his wrists a couple of times, but he ignored her and thought about tomorrow. There would be the funeral arrangements—caskets and flowers and plans for the service. He had lots of experience with that kind of thing. And once her mother was in the family plot over in Mt. Zion Cemetery, Verna would be no problem at all.

On the bed the old woman stopped twitching. He took the pillow away. She stared up, a fixed gaze, her eyes glassy in the moonlight. He thumbed the lids down and straightened the bed.

Should he wake up Verna?

Nah, let her alone.

He smoothed the thin, white hair and patted the cooling cheek. There was no hurry. The old lady would keep.

1

Nola Douglas gripped the armrest as the Chevy Beretta bounced over the gravel road. She should never have let Chuck drive. He sat with a couple of fingers hooked on the steering wheel, supremely confident, while the rental car hit every pothole with teeth-jarring rattles.

At thirty-two Chuck Skaron's baby face still got him carded in bars. He had grown a beard in order to look his age. This morning the growth made him look scraggly and warm.

"Well, where is it?" he asked as they started up a low hill that Nola recognized as the levee.

"In a second."

Chuck barreled over the top and there was the Mississippi, a mud-brown span of water looking more like a lake than a river. In midstream a small boat pushed a string of coal-filled barges south toward Memphis, bright June sunlight dancing on the moving V of the wake. Across on the Tennessee side, the land was flat and featureless.

As they plunged down the levee at breakneck speed, Nola said, "For God's sake, slow down. This isn't the Hollywood Freeway."

"You're telling me," Chuck said. "Where the hell is this place anyway?"

Nola looked for a familiar landmark, depending on her memory and Aunt Vee's directions. It had been fifteen years since Nola had visited Painter's Island, and then she'd come with her grandmother. She remembered houses and cultivated fields, not this dense tangle of vines and rank weeds.

"Well?" Chuck said.

"I don't know. Let's go a little farther."

Ever since Nola arrived two days before for her grandmother's funeral, she had been thinking about the island. No, not true. She had been thinking about the place for months now, long before Aunt Vee called to say that Dorothy Douglas had died in her sleep. Maybe it was precognition . . . except Nola's thoughts hadn't been about her grandmother.

The road turned to parallel the river. Clumps of scrubby willows grew on the wild, sandy shore. The only sign of human habitation was the rusting hulk of a car, buried in the undergrowth. Just when she was sure they had made the wrong turn off the county highway, the main body of the river curved eastward to work its way around a cluster of islands and sandbars, leaving behind a network of sloughs.

Then Nola saw the store. Old and rundown, it sagged under a dusty catalpa. A large metal sign said LIQUORS in huge letters. Almost as an afterthought, somebody had written *Groceries* in green paint on the window.

"Wow," Chuck said. "Civilization."

A man watched them from the doorway. A skinny gray dog stood up from his vantage point by a front stoop, stared, then lay down again, looking as though it was too much trouble to bark.

"Up there." Nola pointed out a road that was little more than ruts in the dirt.

It was another mile before she knew for sure they had

made the right turn. A pontoon bridge spanned a narrow slough that snaked in from the river, defining the island. Beyond the mouth of the slough, three old pilings protruded from the water, all that remained of the boat dock.

Chuck slowed to a cautious creep. The bridge quivered as they rolled across. The shaky, unanchored feeling caught Nola by surprise, then suddenly she remembered the sensation with total recall.

Of course, she'd driven across the bridge many times. She had lived on the island until she was five and had visited every Sunday after her folks moved into town—another three years until her father died and she and her mother left for California. The brain was like a computer, she'd read, with little neurons zapping links into memory storage. Crossing the floating bridge was like pressing the right computer key.

The island was about a mile long, not quite half a mile across, a blob of land that had once been bigger. But the river nibbled relentlessly, depositing bits of the island all the way from Arkansas to the Louisiana delta. Nola rolled down her window and breathed in the rich smells of yeasty earth and standing water.

The trees were third-generation growth, but taller and thicker than she remembered. When Nola was a child, her grandfather had kept the brush under control and there had been more open space. Her mother could keep an eye on her while she dug in the sand along the riverbank or walked beside the inner waterway to look down at the wriggling, restless, teeming life that moved beneath the surface of the dark water.

Now, she caught glimpses of the house, but couldn't see it fully until they rounded a bend and were in the yard.

"Holy shit," Chuck said.

The house loomed in front of them, two stories tall. Dark and ugly, it was built on a high foundation to keep out the worst of the spring floods. The house reminded Nola of a toad frog crouching in the trees. Chuck jumped from the car to stare.

"Jesus, Marvin would love this place," Chuck said.

Marvin Freed had produced the last two horror films Chuck had worked on. Cronenburg out of Corman, was the way Chuck described Marvin.

"I told you it would be a little rundown," Nola said defensively.

"God, it's great. Let's go inside."

Nola climbed the outside steps to the narrow front porch and fumbled with the keys, strangely reluctant to enter. All the memories that had been resurfacing—her mother had told her often enough that she had a vivid imagination. What if that's all it was—just a child's rich fantasies?

One way to know for sure . . .

She turned the key and pushed open the door.

Inside, the air was thick and hot with a dusty, mushroomy smell. Disappointment lumped in her throat. She remembered enormous space and sunny light. Now the living room looked cramped and dim. Yellowed nylon lace curtains hung limply at the dirty windows. Flocked burgundy wallpaper added to the gloom. There was little furniture—a mohair couch, a spindly writing desk, a lamp with dull glass pendants.

She took a few hesitant steps, waiting, expecting—what? Instant recall, she realized, like the feeling earlier on the bridge. Her entire childhood coming back in a rush, fresh and clear in her mind, like an amnesia victim in some old B movie.

Well, it wasn't happening, probably because there was nothing special to remember. She'd been an ordinary little girl growing up in an isolated place. No wonder she had invented an imaginary playmate. Lots of kids do.

You want the memory to be something different,

magical, Nola told herself. She wished she knew why. The real reason, not Dr. Berg's psycho-babble.

Beside her, Chuck spread his hands, creating the box of a camera lens. "I can see it now. Outside—thunder, lightning. Our heroine creeps down the stairs, candle in hand, and sees—creepy music here—the front door—"

"Knock it off," Nola said.

"No, no, I'm on a roll here. The wind's blowing the open door, *thump, thump,* against the wall, and on the door, a big, bloody—"

"Shut *up.*"

Nola headed for the stairs.

"Nola—" Chuck followed her. "Hey, what's your problem, babe?"

"This was my *home,"* Nola said. "Not some damned movie set."

"Yeah, well—I was trying to make a joke. Lighten things up." He looked hurt. "Sorry."

Give him his due, he had stopped off on his way to Detroit. He'd skipped the funeral, but then he'd been up front about his aversion to coffins and burials. Special effects were one thing to Chuck and reality quite another.

"I'm sorry if I snapped at you," Nola said. "Look, why don't you go down and get out the cooler. I'll be right there."

"Okay. I could use a beer."

After he left, she stood there on the landing, feeling the silence settle like dust. She'd never told Chuck about her childhood. Even after living with him for a year, she still couldn't discuss it. In the beginning they were wary of all entanglements, particularly emotional. Chuck still was. Just mention the "C" word—*commitment*—and she could see him mentally reaching for his silver cross and garlic.

What was holding them together? Sex, mainly. Habit. Practical things like the cost of renting a condo in Westwood. Wonderful basis for a relationship.

The truth was she never felt secure enough to trust Chuck with her memories. Which was just as well. She could imagine the number he'd do on that subject.

Depressed, she took a quick look inside the bedrooms. More dust. Mouse droppings. She might as well have wandered into a set on Universal's back lot. Nothing looked or felt familiar.

She went back downstairs. There was still the kitchen, but why bother? Through the open front door she could see Chuck leaning against the Chevy, sipping a Bud Light, glancing impatiently at his watch.

Outside, she pulled the door closed and went down the steps. Disappointment—but more than that, a kind of grief settled in her chest.

"Just another way of running away," Dr. Berg had said when Nola talked about how much she longed to go back home. Of course Nola hadn't told him the whole truth about why she wanted to go. Nola could imagine what her shrink would say about that.

Well, not to worry, doc. Painter's Island was a bust.

So where did that leave her? She'd never been close to her aunt, and now there was Verna's boyfriend hanging around. Frank Moser was skinny, monkey-dark, always watching Nola with his flat, muddy eyes.

"What now?" Chuck asked.

"We came for a picnic," Nola said. "Come on."

She led the way through the overgrown backyard that was littered with debris: a pile of old boards, a rusty abandoned lawn mower, a lawn swing propped against the side of the house. She carried a grocery sack that contained paper plates and napkins, a checkered tablecloth, potato chips. Chuck followed with the cooler.

"What's that?" Chuck pointed at a big earthen mound with a door in it.

"Storm cellar," Nola said. "Tornadoes come up the river like a bowling alley."

Nola watched her step carefully. What would Chuck do if she told him about the snakes? Most were harmless, but there were also copperheads, cottonmouths and water moccasins in these woods. Chuck would freak out of course. He liked his horrors in 70mm up on a nice, safe screen.

At the edge of the river the sandy shore had shrunk, too—or maybe she was just used to Malibu. They sat on a tree stump in the shade and ate cold chicken. Sunlight dazzled off the water, and the air had a damp, viscous quality.

"Who was the artist?" Chuck asked.

"What?"

"You said this place was called Painter's Island."

"Oh." She wiped her hands and sipped her Pepsi. *"Painter* is really *panther* pronounced with a southern accent."

"Panther?" He looked at the woods, uneasy. "Around here?"

"Not now. But a long time ago there were big trees along the river and lots of animals." Her great-grandfather had worked for one of the logging companies that denuded the Mississippi Valley and shipped the lumber north to build St. Louis and Chicago.

"No kidding." Chuck had already lost interest. He mopped his head with a paper napkin and slapped at a mosquito. "I don't know about you, but I've had about enough of this backwoods shit for one day."

At the car she left him to put the cooler and the paper sack in the trunk and went to lock up the house. A waste of time to come here, she supposed. But she had, at least, put her little phantom playmate to rest. Now she could get back to the real world. Her job of putting illusion on the movie screen. Her life with Chuck.

So lock the damned door and be done with it.

She inserted the key in the deadbolt—hesitated—

took it out again and went inside. Dust motes danced in a shaft of weak sunlight.

Give it up, she told herself.

But she knew the fact that she had skipped the kitchen would keep on bugging her, so she went inside.

Standing in the doorway, looking around, she felt that internal sigh of memories slipping into place. A big room, the kitchen had been used for meals too. A round maple table stood in the corner. The big old fireplace had been built at a time when fireplaces were used for cooking as well as warmth. A faint line marked the blackened stones about a foot up, a watermark from the one flood that had inundated the house back in 1919. A rocking chair sat beside the hearth, maple with a spindle back, a small wooden footstool in front of it.

She remembered . . .

Being rocked.

Rocking . . . herself so small, holding someone even smaller.

Playing here, using the footstool for a table. A tiny tea set, dishes for two . . .

A *presence,* warm and comforting. Nothing physical and yet not an imagined friend called up out of loneliness. Something so real—*somebody* so real—what was her name?

All those layers of memory to peel away . . .

Nola sat on her heels and touched the footstool, remembering the tiny china pot, white with blue flowers, the thimble-sized cups.

She had assumed that everybody else knew about her shadowy friend, but that somehow the subject was one of those things not talked about—like breasts and privates. When she slipped and mentioned it, Grandma had been tolerant enough, but her mother and Aunt Vee acted swiftly to put a stop to what Mom called, "this nonsense."

Even when Nola finally realized the strange blindness

10

of adults, she never doubted. She didn't now. Joy welled as she felt the faint prickle in the back of her brain.

"Annie?" she whispered.

No image, there never had been. Just the sense of her, of Annie—Nola remembered her name now—something like fingertips brushing Nola's cheek. But real.

Very real.

2

Annie . . ."

B.J. looked around, startled. The rest area swarmed with people, but none of them was close enough to whisper the name. It was just *there,* an eerie echo in her head.

Her heart gave a sick little lurch at the thought. She felt something sticky oozing between her fingers—the sandwich she was making, clenched in her hand, dripping peanut butter and raspberry jam on the picnic table. She grabbed a paper towel and wiped at the mess.

What the hell was wrong with her anyway? For days now she had felt an itch along her spine as though somebody were standing behind her, and if she looked over her shoulder or turned fast enough . . .

She shivered and licked jam off the back of her hand. Feeling watched was one thing, but voices in her head— *Jesus.*

Maybe it was a *real* echo from somebody out in the parking lot, the sound bouncing off the rest rooms in some weird way. Or maybe the fillings in her teeth had started picking up Memphis radio. Well, it was possible. She had read about it in "Dear Abby."

She scraped the last of the peanut butter from the jar, spread it on a piece of bread, and looked around for Denny. He was nine, much too old for her to take him into the ladies' room; young enough so that she felt apprehensive about him going to the men's room alone.

In the parking lot a big semi chugged past, leaving a scent of diesel smoke. Somebody was cooking hot dogs on a small grill. B.J. smelled a nearby trash barrel, ripening in the hot sun.

She wasn't exactly a rose herself. Her short hair felt damp on her neck, and the edge of her tank top was wet with sweat. A scrawny tree did little to mitigate the heat and nothing to help the humidity. What was that song— something about mad dogs and Englishmen?

Maybe the sun had fried her brains. All she needed to do was put air-conditioning in the truck and move to Colorado. Instant cure for vibrations and voices.

She put Denny's sandwich on a paper plate and waved away a fly. Just when she was ready to pick out some nice middle-aged couple and ask the husband to go check on Denny, her son trotted around the corner. He was lean and lanky like B.J. with a thatch of brown hair already streaked by the sun and a big scab on one elbow.

"I was beginning to think you fell in." She tried for humor but the words came out sharp-edged.

"I had to wait," Denny said defensively. "Can I have a root beer?"

"I'll get it. Eat."

She went off to the camper and returned with two cans of pop from the small refrigerator, pressing hers against her forehead before she pulled the tab.

"Aren't you eating anything?" Denny asked.

"I'm not hungry."

He watched her, sober and worried, as he worked on his sandwich. In the sunlight his eyes were the speckled green of water over stones. His daddy's eyes. Thank God they were the only thing about Denny that reminded her of Chet.

13

Mostly she had forgotten Denny's father. But once in a while her son would glance at her, and she'd remember Chet's dreamy gaze while he talked about signing on a tramp steamer headed for Singapore or getting a job on an oil rig in Saudi Arabia. So many plans—and none of them included marriage and a baby.

She drained her Coke and began putting the picnic supplies back in the cardboard box and picking up the trash. "You about finished?"

Denny nodded and stuffed the rest of his sandwich in his mouth as he followed her to the Toyota.

B.J. had left the windows rolled down in the camper truck, but the cab smelled of hot vinyl, and she had to sit on a towel to keep the seat from burning the back of her legs. Once they got rolling, the breeze blowing through the open windows helped a little. Still, she felt the muscles in her lower back, tight as rubber bands, and she was glad to reach the exit at Arbutus an hour later.

Arbutus was typical of the small Arkansas towns isolated by the Interstate.

"Looks like the drugstore's gone," Denny said.

The windows of the vacant store were empty and dirty. Next door a grocery was still open for business, but the building had a saggy, crumbling look, and B.J. thought it would be the next to close. The main street reminded her of wilting blossoms on a dying vine.

They drove past a small café, a gas station, the Baptist Church. B.J. parked on the street under a canopy of big old oaks. A woman came out of one of the boxy houses, waved, and went back inside—to call the neighbors, B.J. hoped.

"Let's get set up," B.J. said to Denny.

By the time they opened up the camper and B.J. took out her toolbox, two boys pedaled over on their bikes, and people began to drift by. A few came just to talk, but others brought a broken toaster, a useless lamp, a round Hoover vacuum cleaner. B.J. had never studied electronics, never even finished high school, but she had a knack for repairing things, and the people who lived in the small towns hadn't converted to a throwaway society yet.

The circuit every summer was the next best thing to a vacation. They had worked out a regular route: through Arkansas from Little Rock to Memphis, a break to visit her mother, then back down through Tennessee and Mississippi along the river on old Route 61 all the way to Greenville before they returned home. B.J. made enough money for expenses with a little extra to deposit by mail into their savings account.

Besides providing cramped living space, the camper held B.J.'s toolbox and an assortment of wires, cords, and plugs. While she worked on the toaster, Denny took out some folding lawn chairs for the small group that had gathered. One woman contributed iced tea; another, pecan cookies dusted with confectioner's sugar.

The women had a curious, ageless appearance that reminded B.J. of her mother. Family historians and keepers of secrets, B.J. thought wryly. Just like Mama.

After the boys had a snack, they went off to play. The women settled in to tell B.J. about the schoolhouse burning down in Dellwood on New Year's Eve, about the minister passing away in his sleep last month. In return, she told them that Denny had done well in school this year, and, no, she hadn't found a boyfriend.

When her customers went off to make supper, B.J. said good-bye and promised to stop again next summer. Her earnings totaled twenty-two dollars plus a cake from Mrs. Prell—a mini-bundt from the microwave instead of the homemade Tunnel of Fudge Mrs. Prell used to make. Progress, B.J. thought gloomily.

She hoped they would do better in Dellwood. When they left Little Rock, she had bought two hundred dollars' worth of traveler's checks—their emergency fund—and paid for furniture storage, leaving them almost flat broke. They had to give up the apartment in

April and had been living in the camper since then. At this rate she'd never save enough to afford a new place this fall.

Cupping a hand to shade her eyes, she looked up and down the street. No sign of Denny. No sign of anybody on the densely shaded lawns and sidewalks.

She closed her toolbox and folded the chairs. The fine hair on her neck rose, and she stood there, facing the camper, gripping a metal chair frame. One of the women must've forgotten something and come back to get it. If B.J. just turned around . . . but she couldn't because she knew the street was empty, that nobody was there— *nothing* was there—and somehow that was worse. B.J. found herself wishing for a ghost, a two-headed monster, *anything,* no matter how scary, would be better than nothing.

The fear left as suddenly as it had come. She chuffed out a little explosive breath and leaned against the camper, her calf muscles flaccid. She remembered an article in the *Commercial Appeal* last Sunday about schizophrenia. Paranoia, delusions—*voices*—

"Hey, Mom." Denny arrived, riding double with one of the boys on his bike. They skidded to a halt, and Denny said, "'Bye, see you later," as he leaped off.

"Denny, for God's sake." B.J. tossed in the chairs and slammed the camper door. "Where have you been? Get in the truck. Now."

He obeyed, saying nothing until they were driving out of town. "What's wrong, Mom? You getting cramps or something?"

"No, I've got a headache from standing around in the sun waiting for you."

"But it wasn't that late, Mom."

"Denny, please don't argue. Give it a rest, okay?"

She saw the hurt look on his face before he turned away to stare out the window. Dammit, this was nuts—no, scratch that. Stupid. It was stupid. There was no history of mental illness in her family.

Well, there was Great-aunt Delsey. Mama used to say Aunt Delsey was "strange," lowering her voice when she said it and looking around as though somebody might hear. Of course, if B.J. really wanted to worry, there was always the possibility of a brain tumor or a series of little strokes choking off the blood supply to her brain.

Up ahead a sign said: DELLWOOD, NEXT RIGHT. She kept her speed up.

"Mom—"

The exit flew past.

"Mom, you missed the turnoff."

"I thought maybe we ought to go on up and visit Grandma," she said.

"Today?"

"Why not?"

"But we never do it that way," Denny said, bewildered.

"So we do something different this time. We'll surprise Grandma."

"I don't think she likes surprises."

He was right. Of course, Mama would be happy to see them, but she liked to plan things, to have all the events in her life happen in neat and orderly fashion. If they didn't, Iris Johnson would be out-of-sorts and snappish. B.J. didn't care. Tonight she just wanted to sleep in her mother's house.

"Mom?" Denny watched her apprehensively. "Are you okay?"

"Of course. I'm fine."

"You'd *tell* me if something was wrong?"

"Yes, Denny, I would."

"Well," he said, reluctantly persuaded. "Grandma'll be at work, so we'll have to go there. I can see how the animals are doing."

Iris worked at a restaurant out on Route 78, a tourist trap complete with a handful of wild animals and a few domestic ones for kids to pet.

"Sure," B.J. said. "We're just taking our break early this year, that's all."

17

She smiled at him, her face aching with the effort. *Oh, Lord, don't let anything be wrong with me, because if there is—oh, Denny . . .*

Cut that shit out, she told herself. She'd been working too hard. It was too hot. *Nothing was wrong.*

"Annie?"

She gripped the steering wheel. Her palms felt slick, and pain needled in behind her eyes as the low afternoon sun glared on the shiny metal gasoline tanker just ahead.

No mistake this time.

Not a radio signal coming in on her fillings, and it sure wasn't Denny speaking to her. The ghostly whisper was inside her head, faint but clear. It didn't matter that her name was Bethany Jean, and she'd never been called Annie.

The voice was calling to her.

3

Ward Trager opened the pasture gate, and the two frightened Merino sheep bolted through. They raced off into the thin mist that had rolled in from the river, their fat bodies looking like dirty gray blobs in the twilight.

Behind Ward, Ebbie, the Pygmy goat, bleated in alarm. A skinny, sharp-boned, five-year-old girl had the little goat backed into a corner of the petting zoo area. Her older, pudgy brother chased a Banty rooster around the small enclosure while the parents yelled encouragement and recorded everything with a video camera.

The zoo closed at nine, so there were still twenty minutes of torture left for Ebbie. Al Norris wouldn't mind if Ward closed early, but Raylene would ream his ass for sure.

Ward leaned against the fence, feeling the pattern of the cool chain-link squares against his back through his sweaty shirt. The river mist didn't help the heat at all. It just added more humidity.

He thought longingly of the shower he had rigged up behind the enclosure—a garden hose with a stall fashioned from pieces of tin roofing. The cold water would feel good right now.

Off to the right, atop the squat, rectangular Crossroads Restaurant, a huge arrow read *Café*, the word outlined in neon that flashed downward to target the entrance. Big fluorescents illuminated the parking lot and the zoo, each light haloed with a frantic, boiling cloud of gnats, mosquitoes, and June bugs. The light bulbs were freckled by the roasting bodies of the insects giving off a resiny smell. The aroma of frying catfish poured from the kitchen vents and mixed with the pungent odor of fresh sheep manure.

There were still plenty of cars in the lighted parking lot: tourists who preferred to stay off I-55, fishermen from Reelfoot Lake, and a few locals who had dropped by to top up their cholesterol levels. Almost every entrée made a trip through the deep fat fryer, and the menu proudly announced that pie crusts were made with 100 percent pure lard.

Next to the restaurant a billboard pointed the way to the zoo, promising: LIVE! WILD! ANIMALS! SNAKES! TARANTULAS! ALLIGATORS! WOLVES! For all that hype visitors got four cages containing two venomless rattlers, a torpid boa constrictor, three big fuzzy spiders, and a lone timber wolf named, naturally, El Lobo. The alligator had died years ago.

Ward heard a rustle of uneasy movement from the cages as Ebbie bleated louder. Big brother had given up on the rooster and joined his sister in tormenting the goat.

Their mother issued orders directing things for the camera. "That's it, Jocelyn. Keep him making that noise. Don't just stand there, Jason. Move around. Do something."

Jason did. He climbed on Ebbie's back. He had at least forty pounds on the little goat. Ebbie's slender back legs buckled. Ward crossed the pen swiftly, grabbed the boy, and lifted him off the animal.

"That's it for tonight, folks." The girl shrieked a

protest as Ward expertly pried her fingers from Ebbie's chin whiskers. A freed Ebbie stumbled away.

"Hey!" the boy said. "Mom!"

"What do you think you're doing?" Mom demanded.

"Sorry. I'm closing now."

"Well, you can't do that." She turned to her husband. *"Elliot."*

"It's not time yet," Elliot said. "The sign says you're open until nine."

Ward knew he ought to bullshit them. Gee, mister, I'm afraid the big, bad animals might hurt your sweet little kiddies. Instead, he said, "It's close enough," opened the gate to the parking lot, and stood, waiting.

"Wanna pet the goat, Mommy. Wanna *pet* him," the girl wailed.

The woman glared at Ward. In the harsh lighting her skin was bluish white; her hair witchy black. "We're going straight over to talk to the manager. The way you grabbed my children—you'll be lucky to have a job."

Ward said nothing.

"You'll be lucky if—" She broke off, sudden fear in her eyes as they locked with his.

I could burn you down, lady. I could turn you into fucking candlewax.

"Yeah, we're going to report this, all right," Elliot said, just warming up. "Let them know how you're treating their customers."

"Wanna stay, Mommy. Wanna—"

"Shut *up."* The woman dragged her kids through the gate. "Come on, Elliot."

"What do you mean? I'm not letting him get away with this. I said I'm going to see the manager, goddammit."

"Forget it." An edge of panic in her voice. "Let's just *go."*

They piled into an Astrovan with Illinois plates and headed north, back to the Land of Lincoln.

Ward put out the CLOSED sign and switched off the

lights in the cages. He wasn't taking a chance on any more last-minute customers like Elliot and the witch lady and their little brats.

The rattlers moved restlessly, heads up, weaving back and forth. Sometimes Jerry, the cook, brought mice he'd trapped in the storeroom, but the restaurant had been vermin-free this week, so the snakes had eaten only hamburger. The lack of live food made them cranky.

Ward went to unload a bale of hay from Al's old Chevy Luv pickup. Earlier today he'd made his once-a-week trip into town for supplies and a visit to the Laundromat. Shortly after he was hired, Al insisted that he apply for a driver's license and had called a drinking buddy down at the license bureau to make sure Ward had no trouble using the Crossroads as his permanent address on the application.

After the livestock were fed, Ward used a long pole to flip up the latch and push open a door at the back of the wolf's cell. The door opened onto a small run, four feet wide and fifteen feet long, the top covered over with chicken wire. A chunk of gristly beef from last night's feeding lay at the end of the run, mostly uneaten, covered with flies.

Ward figured the wolf would be starved by now, but the animal made no move toward the food. He just crouched, a motionless gray shadow, in a corner of the cage.

"Gotta eat, Bo," Ward said.

Lobo stayed put, staring at Ward, white-ringed irises reflecting wild slivers of light.

Figuring maybe old Bo just didn't want an audience, Ward turned off the rest of the lights, padlocked the gate, and crossed the parking lot to the restaurant. He went inside to a blast of frigid air. Raylene Norris was a stickler for cleanliness, so counters and tabletops shone, but there was always an underlying odor of old grease and stale tobacco trapped by the low ceilings and poor ventilation.

At the cash register Iris Johnson counted out change for an older couple and added, "Ya'll come back to see us now." Iris was in her fifties, short and stout with the kind of figure that was only achieved with an old-fashioned panty girdle made of heavy elastic and a full-figure brassiere. She glanced at Ward, lips thinning in distaste, and looked pointedly at the clock.

8:58.

Raylene sat at a booth in back tallying receipts. She didn't look up, but he didn't fool himself that she didn't notice. The woman never missed a thing. She had threatened to fire him at least once a week since he arrived last March. He figured it was only a matter of time until she carried out the threat.

He headed for the men's room through racks of postcards and standing shelves loaded with corncob pipes and moonshine jugs along with coasters, ashtrays, and paperweights claiming to be made of "real cypress knees" from Reelfoot Lake.

In the bathroom he washed his face and hands, avoiding the mirror. In the past when he looked at his reflection, he'd seen little Flash Trager, fourth-grade skateboard champion, with skinned elbows and a gap-toothed grin and a mania for liver sausage and onion sandwiches. Or the gangling teenager who'd grown a foot in a year and discovered girls, who agonized nightly over whether he'd play for the Lakers or Knicks when he got out of college. Then there was Private Trager, fresh out of boot camp, with his cropped head and bursting energy.

Gone, all of them. They'd died in the rice paddies and bamboo cages somewhere north of Da Nang. And in their place stood a tall, wiry stranger who wore army surplus fatigues because they were cheap and familiar, who had sunbaked skin, long hair tied in a ponytail with an old leather shoelace, and eyes that mostly looked over and around people because when Trager really focused on somebody, he would scare the hell out of them.

He dried his face and tossed the paper towel into the trash. Maybe he could tempt the wolf with fresh game. There were squirrels in the woods, muskrats in the river. This Ward Trager was a specialist in tracking and killing people.

Taking a muskrat would be a snap.

4

B.J. didn't have a key to her mother's house. She knew the place would be locked up tight, so she drove through Dyersburg up to the Crossroads. A night breeze blew through the open windows, cool and pleasant. The thick grass along the side of the road had just been cut, so the air had a rich, green smell. Insects pelted the windshield with a constant *snap snap* that sounded like rain.

The long hours of driving had taken their toll. B.J.'s shoulders ached, and her spine felt bruised from the hard bench seat. Either the voice in her head had gone off to bug somebody else, or it had been some weird radio transmission after all. Denny was right. She should've stuck to her schedule and not come rushing up here.

Too late now. Up ahead the lights in the Crossroads parking lot glowed, oasislike, in the dark country night.

"Do you think the zoo'll still be open?" Denny squirmed, confined by the seat belt and hating it.

"I don't know. Maybe. You're not to make a pest of yourself, Denny. You hear me?"

"Aw, Mom, Mr. Norris likes me."

"Denny—"

"Okay, okay."

He sat up to stare out the front window as they approached the restaurant and said, disappointed, "The zoo's closed anyway."

Just as well, B.J. thought. The animals were like a magnet, their pull too great for a nine-year-old to resist.

Inside the restaurant a few customers lingered, drinking coffee. Iris cleaned the front of the glass case where the cash register sat and kept an eye on a couple browsing through the souvenir racks. When she saw B.J. and Denny, her face lit with happiness, the glow quickly doused by consternation and anxiety.

"Grandma!" Denny ran and threw his arms around Iris's waist.

"Denny—B.J.—what in the world are you doing here?"

"Nice to see you, too, Ma," B.J. said.

Iris gave Denny a little pat, then backed away and withdrew behind the cash register. There was a proper time and place for everything. Work was no place for hugs.

"I wasn't expecting you for two weeks," Iris said. "What is it? What's wrong?"

"Nothing. An impulse—"

"Hey, hey!" Al spotted them and came around from behind the counter. "Look at this one, will you? He's growing like a weed." He tousled Denny's hair and winked at B.J.

"Hey, Mr. Norris," Denny said. "How's all the animals? How's old Lobo?"

"Fine. Fine." Al Norris was tubby and bald. His potbelly and a nose rosy with broken blood vessels were testimony to the cans of Hamm's he drank continuously throughout the day. "B.J., I swear, you get any prettier, I'm going to be in serious trouble with my wife."

B.J. smiled and said hello. Al was a nice man, good to her mother, generous to her and Denny. He waved them to seats at the counter, poured coffee for her, milk for

Denny, and insisted on cutting two slabs of peach pie. Iris sprayed the clean glass, polishing furiously, and darted anxious glances at Raylene Norris, who sat at a booth in the back with a lean, dark man dressed in Army fatigues.

Raylene was a stringy woman of sixty with short, straight, iron-gray hair and crow-black eyes. B.J. thought the only way Al could remain married to Raylene was to stay jovially drunk. The man across the booth from Raylene ate steadily, saying nothing. Raylene was doing all the talking. B.J. couldn't hear what she was saying. It didn't matter. She could tell Raylene was giving him hell.

Al took the coffeepot and went to make the rounds of the tables. B.J.'s hand trembled a little from hunger as she forked peaches into her mouth. When they stopped at McDonald's in Memphis, she had eaten only a small burger and had given Denny all the fries. The pie was heavy and sweet, slightly stale. B.J. was too starved to care.

As she ate the last bite, Iris quickly whisked the plate away. Getting rid of the evidence, B.J. thought, sipping her coffee. "Who's the guy Raylene's chewing out?" she asked her mother.

"Ward Trager. He's been taking care of the animals, but I doubt he's going to last long. Good thing, too. He gives me the willies."

Squirt, squirt with the Windex on the chrome menu holder, the smell sharp and acidic. Iris watched Denny's methodical progress with his dessert.

"Looks pretty slow tonight, Mama," B.J. said. "Maybe you could take off early."

"Oh, no, I couldn't do that." Iris glanced back nervously toward Raylene. "I work until eleven. I have to close, you know. That's my job."

"Right. Sorry. Why don't you give us the spare key then, and we'll go on over to the house."

"Well—" Iris put away the cleaner and took her purse from beneath the register. "The place is a mess, B.J. The

27

beds aren't made up. The laundry isn't done. If you'd come when you said you were coming—"

"Okay, forget it." At this point B.J. was too tired to care where she slept. The floor would've done just fine. Or the parking lot. One of the cages curled up with the tarantulas. "We'll park in the yard and stay in the truck tonight. Come on, Denny. Let's go."

"But I'm not done yet," Denny protested.

"Oh, for heaven's sake," her mother said. "Of course you're not going to sleep in the truck. Here." She thrust the key toward B.J.

In the back booth Ward Trager was leaving Raylene, taking his dishes with him and heading for the kitchen. In a minute Raylene would probably be coming up to the front. Dealing with the woman was the last thing B.J. wanted to do. She took the key from Iris.

"Denny, we're leaving right now." Her voice brooked no argument.

"Oh, okay." He shoveled in the last bite and hopped down from the stool. "'Night, Grandma." He waved good-bye to Al, who waved back.

"Use the blue-flowered sheets," Iris said. "And don't monkey with the living room lamp—"

"It's on the timer," B.J. finished. "I know, Ma. I'll see you in the morning."

Outside a lopsided moon had risen, skimming the trees, limning the small pasture and the animal cages with hard brilliant light.

"Look, Mom, there he is." Denny detoured around the camper truck and ran toward the fenced enclosure, calling, "Hey, Lobo. Hey, boy."

On the other side of the chain-link fence the wolf loped back and forth in a small run, paying no attention to Denny, moonlight a chill silver on his gray fur. At the other end of the cages, B.J. glimpsed the silhouette of a tall, lean man before he stepped back into the shadows. Trager, she thought. Something about the secretive way he moved caused her to quickly close the distance between herself and her son and grab a handful of Denny's shirt.

"In the truck, buster. Now."

"I'm just looking, Mom. I'm not hurting anything."

"Denny, I'm real close to losing it here, so don't push me, all right?"

"Yeah, okay. 'Night, Lobo," he called to the wolf. "See you tomorrow."

Out on the highway heading south, B.J. thought maybe they ought to swing west, cross the river into Missouri, hit I-55 and keep driving through the night. She could mail Mama's spare key from Vicksburg or New Orleans. No, slipping away now would be just as irrational as coming here in the first place.

She figured she was just a little spooked and a lot tired. She certainly had no business roaming around with Denny in that condition, so she kept driving toward her mother's house.

Later, in her old room in one of the twin beds made up with the blue-flowered sheets, B.J. plunged into a deep sleep. She dreamed she was inside the fenced run, looking out of the wolf's eyes. She ran back and forth, trapped, the wire barriers pressing in. There was no escape.

No escape.

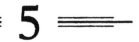

5

After dinner Nola went for a walk around town. Like entering a time machine, she thought. She'd swear the same beds of princess feathers edged the same weedy lawns in front of boxy houses that had been built of rosy brick long before she was born.

Chuck was twitchy with boredom, but he refused to come with her. The picnic on Painter's Island had used up his tolerance for the great outdoors. He wanted entertainment, and he couldn't believe that the nearest movie theater was in Blytheville, a two-plex showing a couple of golden turkeys that weren't worth the drive. He was also flabbergasted by the fact that Aunt Vee didn't own a VCR and didn't subscribe to cable.

"I should say not," Aunt Vee had said when he asked about Showtime or HBO. "All that filthy language. And everybody carrying on like animals."

Chuck settled for watching a baseball game with Aunt Vee and Frank. Nola was just as glad. She had waited all afternoon for a chance to be alone. As twilight deepened into darkness, she reached a field on the edge of town. She remembered rows of cotton here when she was a child. Now the field was full of long grass and tall thistles.

She found a stump beside a fence overgrown with wild honeysuckle and sat down to watch the moon come up. Cicadas sang a deafening chorus, and the heavy, sweet scent of the flowers made her head swim.

Okay, she thought. Okay. No special-effects crew out there on the island today. No cinematic magic. Something really happened.

Something.

But what?

Ghosts, goblins, aliens from outer space—what she knew about the occult came from the kind of movies Chuck and his buddies made, from Stephen King novels, and from tabloid headlines she read while waiting in line at the grocery checkout. Still, this—thing—had to be some kind of paranormal incident. Otherwise, how could she explain it?

And why, she wondered, doesn't it scare the hell out of me?

Maybe because she wanted—needed—something wonderful and unexplainable to happen. She was one of those people who seemed to have everything—brains, looks, talent, success—but underneath was an emptiness she couldn't understand or fill. She tried. Oh, yes, she tried. Her solutions included work, lovers, and, finally, a growing dependence on alcohol that had frightened her into seeing Dr. Berg.

And then, lately, a yearning to come back to Chester had swelled to an ache, and she had begun to think more and more about growing up on Painter's Island, remembering how she'd felt back then.

There had been a sense of family, of course. Daddy, Grandma—all of them together. But there was something else, too.

Annie . . .

She hugged her knees to her chest, chilled in the warm, fragrant darkness.

God, let it be a ghost. A sweet spirit, a wandering angel. Because if it wasn't . . .

No, wait a minute. If you think you're crazy, you can't really *be* crazy, wasn't that the rule?

Annie was real. *I think she was real.* But Nola wasn't sure anymore. Memory—or Memorex? She knew there was only one way to find out.

When Nola let herself in the front door, the ten o'clock news was on, listing the daily toll of doom and disaster. Chuck, sprawled on the couch, gave her a glazed look.

Aunt Vee sat in a wing-back chair licking envelopes. She was plump, pillow-shaped, with fair, unlined skin that she protected religiously with sunscreens and straw hats. In the light from a floor lamp, her scalp looked pink beneath fine blond hair.

"Where in the world have you been?" she asked. "I could've used some help with these." She held up the stack of envelopes. Thank-you notes, Nola knew, for the floral avalanche at Grandma's funeral.

"Sorry, Aunt Vee. I lost track of the time."

Verna sighed. "I swear, Nola, you'd think you were still seven years old, walking around with your head in the clouds."

"Funerals are hard on everybody," Frank said. "Anyway, it's plain to see Nola's not seven anymore. She looks just like your mother, Verna. Did you ever notice that?"

"I suppose so," Verna said. "A little."

"No, no. The spitting image."

He appraised her from Grandma's old leather recliner, his sly gaze like a slug trail over her body.

She wanted to yell, "What the hell are you doing in my grandmother's chair?" She wanted to give Chuck a kick in the ribs because he just sat there and didn't say a word.

The strength of her anger shocked her. To cover it, she turned away and headed for the kitchen, murmuring something about a glass of milk.

Jeez, the man bugged her. Of course, there were plenty of old framed pictures around the house, so it was natural for him to notice Nola's resemblance to her grandmother. And what was Chuck supposed to do— chew the guy out for being observant?

Verna had mentioned Frank Moser in her letters and occasional phone calls, but Nola had never imagined that he was more than a handyman and gardener. He didn't sleep in the Douglas house—at least not with Nola around. Officially, he had a room over at Miss Hopper's, but he spent every waking minute here with Aunt Vee, and the way he touched things, the way he insinuated himself into every conversation suggested more than casual familiarity.

He acts like he owns the damned place, Nola thought, as she moved things in the refrigerator so she could get to the milk carton.

Everybody in town who came to pay their respects had arrived with food: whole hams, chicken casseroles, bowls of ambrosia, coconut cakes, a pecan pie. Nola poured some milk, wedged the carton back on a shelf, and sipped the cold liquid.

Maybe she was just blowing this business with Frank out of proportion. She did have a couple of other things on her mind. Anyway, where did she get off passing judgment on her aunt's choice of men? She'd had some winners of her own, and, face it, Chuck wasn't exactly a prize. After all these years of looking after an invalid, Aunt Vee was lucky to find somebody. So Frank wasn't Paul Newman.

But did he have to be Bela Lugosi?

Nola wished she could talk to her mother about him. She wished her mother were here, dammit. But Faye Douglas—funny how Nola still thought of her mother as a Douglas even though she lost the name three marriages ago—Faye was off honeymooning in the Far East. Nola caught up with her in Hong Kong, but she didn't expect Faye to cut her tour short for the funeral. There had never been any love lost between Faye and her mother-in-law.

From the living room came the strains of the opening

music for the "Tonight" show. Nola finished the milk and washed the glass. As soon as Johnny Carson finished his monologue, she knew Aunt Vee would announce, "It's about that time," and turn off the television. It would never occur to her aunt that anybody might want to stay up any later.

Right on cue the TV went off. Chuck came stomping into the kitchen. "Jesus, Nola, she expects me to go to bed now. Let's get out of here, babe. There must be someplace the good ole boys go. I'll even listen to Johnny Cash and drink bourbon and branch water."

"I'm tired," Nola said. "Bed sounds good to me."

Alone, she wanted to add, grateful that Aunt Vee had put them in separate rooms. But alone her mind would start running in circles again. . . .

She slid her arms around Chuck, pressed the length of her body against his, and whispered, "Give Aunt Vee about fifteen minutes after the last toilet flush. We'll figure out something to do."

She slipped away and headed for the living room. Aunt Vee and Frank were out on the front porch, the door ajar. When Frank spotted her on her way to the stairs and called, " 'Night, Nola. Sleep tight," she managed a pleasant "Good night," but she pictured him with vampire fangs and a ghastly white face. Poor Aunt Vee.

In bed, waiting in the darkness, she heard Chuck's voice, a baritone rumble from the kitchen below. Aunt Vee was busy in the bathroom. He had to be talking on the phone, and it was no surprise at all to find he had been making arrangements to leave for Detroit first thing in the morning.

He waited until after they made love to tell her. Chuck never took chances with his sex life. "Listen, babe," he said, "why don't you go with me? Come on up to Motown for a few days—we'll have fun."

"I can't. There are still a lot of things to take care of here."

"Like what?"

"Grandma's will—formalities . . . tying up loose ends . . ." *Ghosts.* "They want me back in L.A. on Monday."

Preproduction meetings for a new movie. The idea seemed more farfetched than anything that had happened on Painter's Island.

"Tell you what," she said. "Why don't we make the most of tonight?"

"Like to, babe, but I'm out of here first thing in the morning. Gotta get some sleep." He planted a businesslike kiss on her cheek. "You don't have to get up tomorrow. I'll call you from Detroit."

As he padded off to the door, she thought, insensitive bastard. But she couldn't put any rancor into the thought. Chuck was being Chuck. And she was, to tell the truth, glad he was going.

Because now she could go back to the island alone.

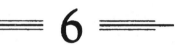

6

True to his word, Chuck was gone in the morning before Nola got up. Aunt Vee was tight-lipped, annoyed by his bad manners, and a little suspicious. Nola thought her aunt had probably already counted the silver.

Nola calculated she might get away to the island by ten. Eugene Lasker, her grandmother's attorney, was due at nine-thirty. Reading the will shouldn't take long.

Frank was in the kitchen when Nola came downstairs. He sat at the breakfast table, chewing his way solidly through fried eggs and slabs of ham. His flat black gaze followed her as she poured orange juice and coffee.

"I see your fellow left," he said. "Thought he was staying for supper."

"He changed his plans," Nola said.

"Don't tell me you two lovebirds had a fight?" He had an oily, knowing smirk in the voice.

She smiled back. "No, Frank. Just the opposite, in fact."

She downed the orange juice at the sink and left, taking her coffee with her into the living room, where Aunt Vee was dusting. Her aunt wore a lavender polyester dress with a big white bow at the neckline, pantyhose, and black pumps. A window air conditioner wheezed, doing little to dint the stuffy closeness. Verna's face shone with perspiration, and she smelled of a mixture of sweat and Chantilly bath powder.

"Aren't you going to change?" A pointed look at Nola's cotton cullottes and tank top.

"No, Aunt Vee. I think I'm fine the way I am."

Nola was too old to be marched upstairs with orders to come back properly dressed. Verna's tight lips and stiff back conveyed her opinion of this laid back California life style.

Nola sat by the window, sipping her coffee, and watched as a big white Lincoln glided into the driveway and parked next to Aunt Vee's dusty black Buick. Verna saw the car too, rushed out to the kitchen to put away the Pledge, and rushed back to open the door before Eugene Lasker had a chance to knock.

Mr. Lasker had been the family attorney for more than thirty years. He was a big man with mild blue eyes and long white hair combed back over his bald spot. His face sagged with a peculiar slackness, as though the skin had come loose from the muscle and bone underneath.

He came into the living room and offered Nola his large, soft hand. He had been at the visitation at the funeral home and, of course, at the services, but he gave his condolences again, accepted coffee, and chatted about what a nice send-off Dorothy Douglas had had.

In L.A. lengthy separations were handled with, "hey, how's it going?" But in Chester, every meeting involved a large amount of ritual conversation. Funny though. This polite waste of time used to drive Nola crazy. Now she found it oddly comforting.

Frank sidled in from the kitchen to offer coffee refills and stayed. At least he had the decency not to sit in her grandmother's chair. He hovered in the background as Lasker finished his coffee and opened his worn leather briefcase.

"This should probably be just family." Lasker glanced at Frank as he extracted legal documents.

"I'd like to have Frank here," Verna said. "Unless Nola minds."

Yes, I mind, Nola thought. But, really, what difference did it make? She shrugged. "It's okay with me."

"Very well, then." Lasker put on a pair of wire-rimmed glasses. "I can read this, give you all the legal language, or I can just tell you what it says in plain English."

"That would be fine," Verna said.

"All right, then. Simply put, Dorothy's estate, all the property and money, is to be split between the two of you, her only living relatives."

Verna gasped. She got the message right away. Nola was a little slower.

She stared at Lasker. "Split? I never thought—Aunt Vee took care of Grandma all these years."

"There's some mistake." There was a thin strident note in Verna's voice. "It can't be."

"I'm sorry, Verna. I know this wasn't what you were expecting, but it's what Dorothy wanted. She felt very strongly about providing for Nola, too." He turned to Nola. "I'm afraid your grandmother had no faith in the security of your job in the movie industry. She wanted you to have something to fall back on."

He went back to the document and flipped a page. "Now, for particulars. Understand, there are no strings here. Either of you can sell any or all the property. Dorothy knew you might want to do that. But in case you didn't, her idea was that each of you have a house and some income. Verna, this house here in Chester is your home and Dorothy wanted you to have it. Nola—"

Nola sat up, her heart drumming.

"Nola, the old homeplace on Painter's Island is yours."

He droned on, but his voice seemed to come to Nola from a long way off through water. It's mine, she thought.

Oh, Grandma . . . Tears welled up, hot and prickly behind her eyes.

She hadn't cried for her grandmother. Not for the frail, querulous old lady who had spent Nola's brief visits complaining about her arthritis and the way the world was going to hell.

Now Nola had a sudden clear memory of the younger, vigorous woman who always had time to mend a toy or go looking for blackberries and crayfish, whose strong arms were sure comfort for scraped knees and wounded pride. And for the first time Nola felt the overwhelming grief of knowing something precious was lost forever.

Wrapped in her private sorrow, Nola heard what Eugene Lasker was saying, but none of the details of mortgages and lease income registered until Aunt Vee cried, "You can't mean—that's all there *is?*"

Twin spots of color splotched Verna's cheekbones, bright red against the pale skin. She hunched her soft shoulders as though warding off a blow, her chin sunk in the big white bow.

Frank moved up to stand behind her chair. His flat, unblinking gaze fixed on Nola's face.

"That can't be right." Verna's voice was reedy with near panic. "There was always money—plenty of money."

"At one time," Lasker said patiently. "But there's been a steady erosion of capital, Verna. Still, if you're careful, there's no reason you can't go on living here quite comfortably."

"How do you know I *want* to live here? How do you know I don't *hate* this awful old house—and this town—and—"

"Verna," Frank said sharply and gripped her shoulder.

Her mouth worked, but he'd effectively stopped the hemorrhage of words.

"She's just tired," Frank said. "Taking care of her mother day and night, and then the funeral and all. She's exhausted and upset."

"Well, of course," Lasker said. "I'm sorry this is such a trying time for you, Verna. I'll just leave these—" He laid two copies of Dorothy Douglas's will on the coffee table. "You can read over everything when you're up to it. Think about what you want to do. When you're ready, call me."

Verna sat, stunned and solid, so Nola walked Lasker to the door, murmuring thanks.

"Don't forget one thing, my dear," he said softly. "This was your grandmother's estate, and her privilege to dispose of any way she wanted."

After he left, Nola stood in the entryway for a minute, her own elation subdued by her aunt's reaction. If the will had been a shock to Nola, imagine what it had been like for Verna. Nola had been eight years old when her father died, and she and her mother moved to California. After that, her childhood ties to her father's family had slowly weakened. Distance wasn't the only barrier between L.A. and Chester, Arkansas.

Nola had expected a small sum of money. She was unprepared for her grandmother's generosity . . . and Aunt Vee's resentment.

In the living room Verna still crouched, shoulders hunched. Moisture sheened her face, and her ankles were puffy in the tight pumps. Frank had pulled up a side chair and sat beside her, leaning forward, his head close, speaking quietly. He broke off as Nola came in.

"Are you all right, Aunt Vee?" Nola asked. "Can I get you something? Some water—or maybe some iced tea . . ."

Verna's head snapped up. Her eyes blazed with hatred, cold and pure as laser light.

"That's nice of you, Nola," Frank said smoothly, "but you don't have to bother. I'll take care of Verna."

Nola backed away, murmured something about needing air, grabbed her purse, and escaped to her car. A block away from the house she had to pull over and stop. She sat there, gripping the wheel, shaken.

My God, Nola thought. Does Aunt Vee really despise me that much?

Surely not. Verna was overreacting to bad news, that's all. But, driving away, Nola wasn't sure that she really believed it, especially when she remembered the look on Verna's face.

7

"Mama, why don't you sit down and let me pour you a cup of coffee," B.J. said. "We can do a little catching up."

. . . and you can tell me just how strange Aunt Delsey really was and if there was anybody else in the family who heard voices and felt like somebody was watching her.

Iris was at the sink, the hot water running. She'd jumped up as soon as Denny ate the last bite of waffle and grabbed his plate.

"You go ahead, help yourself." Iris squirted Joy in the sink, whipped up suds. "You know I can't sit still until after I straighten up."

"Uh-ho," Denny said under his breath. He slipped off his chair and headed for the back door. "Thanks for breakfast, Grandma. Gotta lot of stuff to do in the camper."

"Okay for you, buster," B.J. muttered.

He gave her a wink and ducked out.

Working alongside her mother was not a companionable thing to do. For Iris daily cleaning was all-out war requiring total concentration.

During the next two hours B.J. tagged along as her mother whirled around the house. In Iris's wake, sinks sparkled, furniture and wood floors glowed, and the rooms filled with a haze of pine oil and lemon scents as if Iris had shoehorned a whole artificial forest into the small house.

As soon as Iris finally took off her apron and looked around with a nod of satisfaction, she glanced at the clock, exclaimed that she was going to be late, and left in a run to get dressed for her hair appointment.

B.J. sighed. No use expecting Mama to postpone the trip to the beauty parlor. Might as well ask the moon to try a new orbit. B.J. shivered. Iris's one luxury was the two air conditioners that ran day and night, keeping the house a frigid sixty-eight degrees. Too chilly for B.J. in her shorts and T-shirt.

She took a can of Pepsi from the fridge and went out on the back porch, sat on a vinyl-webbed chair, and propped her bare feet up on the porch railing. Two towering hickories and a maple spread a canopy of leaves over the yard, the dense, green shade already full of drowsy warmth.

Quiet. Peaceful. Maybe this was really all she needed. Just a few days off, a little R and R. Since that episode in the truck she'd been just fine. No voices. No crawl of gooseflesh on her neck. Just, now and then, a kind of quiver inside her head as though somebody had brushed their fingertips across her frontal lobe.

Out on the driveway she could hear the rasp of skateboard wheels, then Mama's voice, warning Denny to mind the traffic before the old Dodge started up and drove away.

Denny trotted around the corner. "Where'd Grandma go in such a hurry?"

"Guess."

He considered. "What day is it?"

"Tuesday."

He grinned and hoisted himself up on the railing, swinging thin, tanned legs. "Was Grandma always like this?"

"Always."

Denny sobered and looked a little sad. "Poor Grandma. I don't think she's had much fun."

"Some people don't. Life hasn't been easy for your grandma."

B.J.'s parents had come from poor farm families. At a time when many young people took off for the cities, they had stayed. Doing all right, as her mother put it, until Everett Johnson had died when his farm truck overturned and fell into the swollen Running Deer River one rainy April day when B.J. was five years old.

Even before she was widowed, Iris always worked, cleaning other people's houses, picking strawberries, running a presser in a laundry. After her husband's death, she just worked twice as hard. Time with her mother had been a precious commodity, but B.J. had never gone hungry, and they always had a roof over their heads, even if it was a leaky one.

"I'm glad Grandma has a good job now," Denny said. "The Crossroads is a neat place. I can't wait to go over to see the animals."

"Denny—"

"I know, Mom. I'm not gonna be a pest. Trust me." He reached for her Pepsi, took a long swallow, and handed back the can. "Is it okay if I go down to the park for a while?"

"I guess so." He was already off and running as B.J. yelled, "don't be late for lunch."

She went out to the camper for a sweater and gathered up some laundry. After she got the wash started, she went into the kitchen and set the table. With luck she'd have a few minutes alone with her mother before Iris left for work. And then what? B.J. had no time to rehearse her questions because Iris arrived with two bags of groceries, smelling of hair spray. Her short, ash-brown bubble cut had been set and lacquered into place—good for another week.

"Cotto salami was on sale." Iris dealt with the bags, handing B.J. food to be stored in the refrigerator. "But then I wasn't sure Denny liked it, so I bought baloney, too. And I got a chicken you can cook for supper. Head lettuce was awful. You wouldn't think head lettuce would be that bad this time of year."

There was more, something about tomatoes, but B.J. wasn't listening. Welts of goose bumps had risen on her neck, and she knew if she turned around real quick—

"B.J.?" Iris said sharply.

"What?"

"Are you feeling all right?" Iris stood, holding out a carton of eggs.

B.J. took the carton. "I'm fine. Just—"

"Annie?"

The voice rang in her head. She felt the egg carton slide from her hands, and stared down stupidly as it hit the floor.

"B.J.! For heaven's sake!"

Thick yellow yolk oozed out on the white tile. Iris grabbed her arm and guided her to a chair.

"What is it?" She put a wrist against B.J.'s forehead. "You're not warm. Are you sick to your stomach? Good lord—" She dropped down on a chair. "B.J., you're not—pregnant again?"

If only this were something as simple and wonderful as a baby, B.J. thought. "No, Ma. I'm not pregnant. I'm—"

"Annie . . ."

B.J. put her fingertips against her temples, pressing hard as though she could squeeze the voice from her head.

"What is it, then?" Iris asked. "A headache?"

"Sort of."

"Migraine, I bet. Your daddy had them. Did I ever tell you that? Lord, how he suffered. Bright speckles in front of his eyes, he used to say, and sick as a dog—"

"Mama, did he ever—did he hear anything?"

"No, I don't think so. You mean like maybe a ringing sound?" Iris jumped up, grabbed a handful of paper towels, and began wiping up the broken eggs. "I read about that. I think it's called tin—tin something. I don't think there's a thing the doctors can do for it."

Denny burst in through the back door. "Oh, boy. I thought I was late for sure." He stopped to stare at B.J. "Mom? Mom, what's wrong?"

"Nothing. I'm all right."

"Your mother has a headache," Iris said. "Why don't you run upstairs and get her some Advil."

"That's okay." B.J. stood up. "I think I'll just go and lie down for a few minutes."

"That's a good idea. Pull down the blinds. That's what your daddy used to do."

In her old room, sitting on one of the twin beds, B.J. tried to remember everything she'd ever read about migraine. Wasn't there something about peculiar smells? She couldn't recall anything about hearing voices, but then she hadn't done a complete study.

She looked around the room. Even though she'd never lived in this house as a child—Mama moved in five years ago—many of the things in the room were B.J.'s: a framed cross-stitched sampler that read *Jesus loves the little children,* a scarred maple dresser, a lamp with pink roses painted on the glass globe, and the white chenille bedspread.

When she was growing up, they had moved constantly, living most of the time in tiny places where she shared a bedroom with her mother. With Iris working they hadn't been together much during the day, but there were all the evenings and nights, and never once had Iris mentioned that Everett Johnson suffered from migraine headaches.

Maybe there were other things Mama hadn't told her. A lot of other things.

8

Nola turned off the county road and drove slowly through the gates of Mt. Zion Cemetery. The caretaker lived near the entrance in a sagging old house with a shed alongside for storing equipment. Enormous sunflowers nodded by the front door. Pole beans grew up a fence. Chuck could make something of that—fleshy roots snaking underground, seeking out coffins—but she doubted that the caretaker gave it much thought. She could see him off in the distance cutting the grass. When she parked and shut off the engine she heard the drone of the mower. The fresh-cut green smell blended with the heady scent of wild honeysuckle that Nola had stopped outside Chester to pick.

Three big black oaks provided shade from the fierce, spongy heat. Her grandmother's grave was easy to spot. The sod was in place, but it looked freshly turned. A few flowers remained, browning rapidly in the sun. The stone was a modest granite slab, identical to the ones on either side marking the graves of Nola's father and her grandfather.

She and Aunt Vee were the only remaining candidates

for the half-dozen empty plots, something Grandma had complained about the last time Nola saw her.

"Don't wait too long to have children," Dorothy had said. "Life plays terrible tricks, then leaves you with nothing."

Nola reached out to touch the sharply incised letters in the sun-warmed granite. DOROTHY DOUGLAS, 1908–1989. Her grandmother was a great believer in families. She had grieved that her own had shrunk so badly. Her will had probably been an attempt to draw Nola back here and reestablish the Douglas line.

Whatever Dorothy's motive, it came from love. Nola hoped, in time, Aunt Vee would realize that. I'll have to try and talk to her, Nola thought. For Grandma's sake.

Meanwhile, she whispered her thanks to her grandmother and left her offering of honeysuckle on the new grass.

This time when Nola opened the door of the old island house, she felt as though she were opening a gift. The rooms were still small, dim, and stifling, but now she saw the hand-carved moldings, the solid oak stair railing, and the leaded sunburst of glass over the front door.

She went to the living room windows, hesitating only a moment before she ripped down the tattered old lace curtains. The wood of the window was swollen and warped, so she had to push hard before the frame came free. Then she opened it wide to let in the river breeze. She went through the rest of the living room and on upstairs, not stopping until the whole house was open. Clouds towered in the west, and the air was warm and sultry, but the freshness cleansed the awful, mushroomy odor.

Her last stop was the kitchen. Ignoring the dust, she sat in the rocker next to the fireplace and mopped her sweaty face on the tail of her tank top. Motes danced in the stream of sunlight from the open window. Outside, leaves rustled and birds sang.

"Annie?" she whispered.

Not a reply—exactly. Just something gathering in the room, a linking . . .

She leaned back and closed her eyes, thinking, I'm home.

Home—maybe that was it. Not little ghosts at all, but a feeling of being part of this place. Her father had been born upstairs in the master bedroom. So had she. She had crawled on this floor, learned to walk here, had fallen and cut her forehead on the edge of the hearth. She still carried the scar.

If her father hadn't crashed on his way to Memphis in a friend's private plane, she would have lived here at least until it was time to go off to college. Maybe she would have been content to marry a local boy and stay, firmly anchored by two generations of roots.

Faye Douglas often talked about the narrowness of her own escape, although Nola wondered if the failure of her mother's next two marriages and her incurable wanderlust was the result of being so suddenly set adrift.

Good thing her mother was in China with husband number four. By the time they returned, Nola would have had an opportunity to think, to make up her mind—about what? Really, there was nothing to decide. She was due back in Hollywood on Monday. Back to the sixteen-hour days, to living on coffee and adrenaline.

She had to go back. Still . . . out there in the cemetery and now here in this house, awash in sunlight and the river smells, she felt separated from the past by the thinnest membrane. Bits and pieces she had heard as a child leaped into vivid scenes.

Raw wood, the smell of sawdust and varnish as the house took shape. The dark, sleek shape of the panther who came the first night her great-grandparents slept here. Joe Douglas's hound baying madly and Joe coming down with the shotgun—standing quietly in the moon-silvered living room and letting the panther slip away. And then that night in 1919 when the river swept through the rooms—children crying and a mule braying, crazed with fear.

I could tell that story, she thought.

Not for the screen. Everybody in Los Angeles was pitching ideas, hyping high concepts, spewing out scripts. This should be shaped by words on the printed page.

The idea of writing a book wasn't new. She considered it a pleasant daydream, something to indulge in when she couldn't sleep, a mental exercise to help endure the tedium of a boring shoot.

I really could do it.

Here. In this house.

The place was a mess, but with a little elbow grease, some paint—Nola looked around. Well, maybe it would take a little more work than that, but it could be done. And then—then she would be out here all alone, just her and her typewriter, and Annie.

Wind gusted suddenly through the open windows, and upstairs a door slammed shut. She smelled the hot-dust, ozone scent of approaching rain and heard thunder in the distance. A stormy darkness came quickly as she raced around, closing up everything.

She wanted to stay, but clouds boiled, an ominous deep purple, and lightning jumped across the sky as though some huge high-tension wire had been left to hiss and spark. Tornado weather, her grandmother would have said, and hustled them all out to the storm cellar.

Outside, rain pelted down, so suddenly and so savagely that she was soaked—clothes and hair plastered to her body—before she could jump inside her car. The pontoon bridge swayed wildly as she rolled across. Shivering, she hunched forward to study the sky through the deluge of water that was barely cleared by the windshield wipers. No sign of a funnel cloud. Her more immediate problem was the dirt road, churned to slippery mud by the rain.

Just a taste of what it would be like to live alone out here. She told herself the whole book thing was a crazy idea. She was already committed to the new movie and semicommitted to Chuck.

Still . . . yes, still . . . a sweet fantasy to dream about as she drove through the rain back to Chester.

Pulling into the driveway in front of her grandmother's house, Nola realized she'd done a good job of putting Aunt Vee completely out of her mind. Maybe Verna had calmed down by now. The will had come as a big shock; naturally it would take her aunt some time to adjust.

More than just an afternoon, Nola thought, remembering the hate in Verna's eyes.

From the look of the sky, the rain wouldn't let up any time soon. No sense waiting. She got out of the car and splashed her way to the front door, soaked again by the time she let herself inside.

Frank sat in the living room, drinking a beer and reading the paper. He looked up, a sly avidity in the black gaze. The way the wet knit fabric clung to her breasts she might as well have been naked, her nipples taut with cold, the large dark areolae plainly visible.

"Better get out of those clothes," he said. "Get into a hot tub."

"That's what I plan to do." She headed for the stairs. "Where's Aunt Vee?"

"Taking a rest. I talked her into going out for dinner. Why don't you come along?"

"Thanks, but I'm expecting a phone call."

"That stopper in the bathtub can be kinda stubborn," he called after her. "If you need any help, just give me a yell."

In your dreams, Nola thought.

After she made sure the door was locked, she soaked in hot water until her teeth stopped chattering, then dressed in cotton slacks and a long-sleeved shirt. She was drying her hair when Frank knocked on the door to say her boyfriend was on the phone.

Frank stood outside in the narrow hall, waiting—

deliberately positioned, she thought, so she had to brush past.

On the kitchen phone Chuck talked a mile a minute. Detroit sucked, he said, heat and humidity—almost as bad as Chester. But the locations were dynamite: filthy, grungy—perfect. "How about you, babe? Climbing the walls yet?"

"Not really," she said. "There's a lot going on. It seems that Grandma left half of everything to me in her will."

"Half, huh?" Unless they were talking Rodeo Drive, Chuck was not impressed. "You think it will be hard to unload?"

"I have no idea."

"Well, you'd better get cracking and find a real estate agent. Maybe you'll net enough for a down payment on the condo."

"Maybe." Assuming she wanted the condo. Assuming she wanted to sell.

She promised to call as soon as she got back to L.A., then hung up. The yellow pages lay on the counter directly under the wall phone. She picked up the directory, sat down on a kitchen chair, and thumbed through the book.

Nothing under *Remodeling. Contractor–Building* yielded a half dozen names. There were more under *Painting and Paper Hangers.*

She tried two of the contractors. Secretaries at both offices told her the same thing. They were pretty busy, and they couldn't give her any quotes until somebody actually looked at the house. If Nola wanted to make an appointment—this week? Not a chance. Sorry.

A third call yielded only an answering machine. She glanced at her watch. It was almost five. The rest of the calls would have to wait until tomorrow.

Frank watched Verna punch the button to shut off the speaker on the phone, her hand trembling, a dull red tide of rage creeping up her face. They were in the old woman's room. Verna was sitting on the bed, and he leaned against the night table where the phone lay.

Frank had gone directly to Verna after telling Nola that Chuck was calling. Verna was a little jittery, but she was no dummy, and she was still mad about what that old bitch had done, splitting up the estate. So he didn't have to coax much to get her to come in here and listen in to Nola's conversations. We just need to know which way the wind's blowing, he told her. We have to make plans.

The speaker phone was perfect. Verna bought it on a shopping trip to Memphis after Dorothy became bedridden and used it like an intercom so she didn't have to run up and down constantly. They turned the volume low, leaned close, and heard every word.

"Lot of good it does," Verna said bitterly after Nola completed her calls. "So we know she's thinking about staying and fixing up that old place. So what?"

"You can't tell. Things can happen," Frank said.

"Something already happened. That stupid will—"

She picked up a pillow, kneaded it as if she were punching dough. Might be the same pillow he had held over old Dorothy Douglas's face, Frank mused. He liked to think it was. The idea hummed in his head and warmed the blood in his veins.

"Maybe we could go to court," Verna said. "The way Mama was toward the end—she was definitely getting senile, wasn't she, Frank?"

"I think so, but I doubt it'll matter. I looked at the papers, Verna. That will was written ten years ago."

"Ten years," Verna said, aghast. "All that time—she knew I expected to get everything, and she never said a word. Just let me clean up her messes and wait on her hand and foot. It's not right. It's just not—not fair—" She broke off as angry tears burst from her reddened eyes.

"Shh, hush, now." He stood beside her, let her lean her head against him, and stroked her hair. It felt a little like Dorothy's had that night—thin and fine.

He could see the old woman's face staring up at him, eyes bugging out, lips peeled back over the purpling gums. Maybe she had been laughing at him, knowing what she did. Knowing that Verna wouldn't get all the money.

And now here was Miss High-and-Mighty Nola. She looked so much like the old bitch it was spooky. Flaunting all that bare skin with those long legs and that perfect ass. She had been surprised to hear about Verna getting shafted, but Frank didn't notice her offering to give up her share. No, sir. She was already making plans to spend Verna's money. His money.

Well, we'll just have to see about that, he thought. He had read the will, and maybe the old lady wasn't so smart after all.

Things can happen, Frank thought. Oh, yes, they surely could.

9

Ward pressed the forked stick down, pinning the diamondback, until he got a good grip on the back of the head. A second snake coiled, rattling furiously. Quickly he slipped the first one into a fabric laundry bag and used the stick to pin number two.

As he lifted the second rattler, Ward looked up and saw the boy standing on the other side of the cage. Sun-streaked hair, serious hazel eyes—it was the same kid who had been in the restaurant last night, and who had rushed over to the zoo later, excited to see the wolf. The boy watched quietly while Ward handled the snakes.

He waited until Ward had both rattlers in the laundry bag and had pulled the drawstring closed to say, "Mr. Simms used to just sort of shove them out of the way. He said the poison stuff had been taken out."

Simms was the name of the last caretaker.

"That's true," Ward said. "But they still have their fangs." Tourists weren't impressed by toothless snakes. "If they bite, it hurts and could get infected."

Ward knew a lot about infections. He carried the scars, lines of lumpy white flesh that ridged his hands.

"Mr. Simms always let me help clean up," the boy said. "I'm Denny Johnson. My grandma works over at the restaurant. What's your name, mister?"

Ward told him.

"I love the tarantulas," Denny said. "They feel so soft. They like to be petted."

"Is that so?" Ward sprayed the inside of the glass snake cage with Windex and wiped it. Rain drummed on the tin roof. Ebbie, the goat, and the two Merinos stood in one corner under the overhang, eyeing the boy nervously. Lobo crouched, motionless, in his cage.

"I could clean up the sheep turds," Denny offered. "I wouldn't mind."

"You wouldn't, huh?"

"No, sir," he said. "It gets awful stinky if you don't keep that stuff picked up."

Ward couldn't suppress a smile as he put down the Windex and passed a shovel and a cardboard box to Denny over the cages. Denny went to work, scooping up dung from under the overhang.

"Mr. Norris said me and my mom should come over for supper," Denny said. "But he's having trouble with one of the ovens, so Mom's taking a look at it first."

"Your mom repairs ovens?"

"She sure does." There was pride in Denny's voice. "My mom can fix anything."

Denny worked his way down the enclosure, taking care not to scare the sheep. When he was finished, he stopped in front of the wolf's cage, saying, "Hey, Lobo, hey, boy."

Ward upended the laundry bag to release the snakes and shut the door to their pen.

"Mr. Trager?" Denny said, worried. "What's wrong with Lobo? Is he sick?"

"I don't know. Could be."

"You let him out at night, don't you? I don't think Mr. Simms did. Not always. Lobo hates being all cooped up."

"Denny!" A shout from the restaurant entrance. A

woman ran across the parking lot, dodging puddles, a big black umbrella over her head.

"It's Mom," Denny said. "Hi, Mom. I'm helping clean up. And I'm not being a pest. Am I, Mr. Trager?"

"You can take the Fifth," his mother said with a rueful smile.

She was tall, slim, but sturdily built, nothing at all like her mother, wearing jeans and a man's plaid shirt rolled up to the elbows. The masculine clothes only emphasized the curve of her hip, the full breasts. She had short hair, a sunstreaked brown like Denny's, brown eyes, and square, competent hands.

"The kid was no bother." Ward's words came out stiff, gruff. He moved down to the tarantulas, putting extra distance between himself and the woman.

"That's good." She turned to Denny. "As for you, buster, I don't like you running off and not telling me where you're going."

"Aw, Mom. You knew I'd be out here."

"Yeah, well, I figured you were, but that's not the point. We'll talk about this later. Now, say good-bye to Mr. Trager and let's go eat."

Denny obeyed, coming over and offering his hand. Ward had to take it, leaning over to grip the small sturdy fingers that smelled faintly of goat manure.

"I'll come help you again tomorrow," Denny called as he rushed off, trailing his mother.

Ward might have said he didn't need any help, didn't want any, but they were gone, running off through the rain.

He waited until Denny and his mother left the Crossroads before he went in to eat. But he mentioned them to Al—casually—and Al told him her name.

"I think it's Bethany but she goes by B.J.," Al said, a wistful lust in his eyes. "Boy, she's a real peach. Got knocked up when she was sixteen. Raised Denny on her own. He's a nice kid, too. I take a personal interest in those two, Trager. You know what I'm saying?"

"Yeah." Ward had a hard time keeping his voice neutral and free of bitterness. "Just curious."

Raylene was busy harassing the busboy, so Ward managed to slip out unnoticed. The rain had stopped. He spread his sleeping bag in back of the cages under the overhang, just in case. Usually he slept at the far end of the pasture, and sometimes Ebbie would come and bed down beside him on the other side of the fence. He always slept better out in the open, even in winter. The cold didn't bother him nearly as much as the feeling of being trapped, of walls shrinking and moving inward.

Before crawling into bed, he made sure the wolf's door was open to the run. The remains of the muskrat carcass was down there, only a few bites eaten, not nearly enough to keep the full-grown timber wolf alive. The animal had to be starving, but he stayed in the cage. Ward was sure he hadn't moved at all.

Lying in the sleeping bag, he could hear the wolf's soft panting. If the beast got hungry enough, he would eat. Ward knew about hunger. The menu at Chez Charlie's had included rotten rice, fish heads, beetles, grubs. In the beginning his stomach rebelled, but there comes a point when the body won't take no for an answer. It insures survival with red-hot pincers in your belly and in your brain, forcing you to swallow.

Even though his stomach was full, he felt a twinge of pain at the memory. Beyond the edge of the lighted parking lot the night moved, awake, restless. He listened to a chorus of frogs and owls and a steady drill of insects. He heard unnamed rustles in the undergrowth. Jungle sounds. Jungle smells, too.

The fucking rain.

He was in the cages again, listening to Remy's moans. Remy Lavauge, the stupid Cajun, who for months wouldn't eat and wouldn't die.

Gotta promise, Trag. Gotta make a pact. One of us can't stand it no more, the other finds a way . . .

Out in the parking lot the big fluorescents blinked off. The last cars left. A throaty roar burst from the Norrises' Mercury and then silence. It was very dark now. Through broken clouds he saw stars and a faint glow of moonlight.

There was quiet movement in the wolf's cage. Lobo had turned slightly, facing toward Ward. Moonlight traced the metal bars and picked out the white-ringed irises. They gleamed eerily, points of dull light in the dark prison.

Jesus, Jesus.

Nothing in the world Ward hated as much as a cage, and now here he was—the keeper.

=== 10 ===

Iris liked a snack when she got home from work, so B.J. got it ready as soon as she heard the car pull into the driveway. A ripe banana mashed and mixed with peanut butter. A plate of club crackers. Decaffeinated tea.

"You didn't have to go to all this trouble," Iris said.

"I didn't mind, Ma."

While Iris ate, B.J. sipped a glass of milk, her stomach clenched so tightly the liquid would barely go down.

Iris edged off her shoes and rubbed her swollen ankles. "I still don't know if I like your working on the oven."

"It wasn't my idea. Al asked me to." This was not, the first time B.J. had repaired something at the Crossroads.

"Still—you know how Raylene is. If something goes wrong, she'll never let me hear the end of it."

"It's not very complicated," B.J. said. "Probably just the wiring. I'll have to bring Denny along, Mama. I don't want to leave him here alone all day. I talked to Al about it."

"Well, if you have to," Iris said reluctantly. "But I do wish you'd keep him away from that Ward Trager."

B.J. had been a little leery of Ward herself that first evening, but she thought she may have overreacted.

"He seems nice enough."

"B.J., he sleeps with the animals. Hardly ever talks. And sometimes, the way he looks at you—it makes my skin crawl. Al says he was a prisoner of war. They can go crazy, you know. The least little thing can trigger them off, and they blow up—just like that."

"I doubt the man has an exclusive on mental problems," B.J. said. "We've had a few in our own family."

"*Our* family? Where did you get an idea like that?"

"Well, there was Aunt Delsey."

"Oh, that was different."

"Was it? You never told me what happened to her, Mama."

"I never liked to talk about it," Iris said. "It was an awful thing. Your Great-aunt Delsey lost her baby, B.J. A little girl, about six months old. April, that was her name. They lived on the Hendrix farm down toward Jackson. Little April was outside, lying on a pallet, while Aunt Delsey worked in the garden. Just a few feet away."

Iris picked up a cracker and spread it with the last of the peanut butter-banana mixture. "Mr. Hendrix had a bull he used for breeding. A great big, mean old bull. He was always getting out of the pasture. That day Aunt Delsey saw him coming. She screamed and ran at him with her hoe, but he threw her out of the way, just lowered his head and tossed her aside. And then he kept going—right toward the pallet."

She put the cracker down on the plate and pushed it away. B.J.'s stomach clenched tighter.

"My God," she said.

"I was about nine years old, but I still remember the funeral like it was yesterday—that tiny little casket. Aunt Delsey was clean out of her head for a long time. She got better, but I don't think she ever got over it."

Iris stood, took her dishes to the sink, and began

briskly putting the kitchen in order. B.J. sat, stunned, her mind still full of the horror of the scene her mother's words had conjured up.

"I think the rain's stopped," Iris said. "It'll be a scorcher tomorrow. Hot and muggy. Brings in a lot of fishermen to the lake, so we'll be busy."

How does she do that? B.J. wondered.

She pictured her mother's mind as full of compartments. When Iris wanted to forget about something, she locked it in its own little cubbyhole, and it was gone. Like now.

Iris rattled on about how there were more mosquitoes because of the rain and how that made the fish bite. Then she segued into a report on her last visit to Great-aunt Mamie, poor old soul. Iris diligently kept track of the remaining relatives, taking them cakes and sacks of hickory nuts from the trees in the backyard. B.J. was sure her mother didn't really enjoy these visits, but she felt an obligation to go, so she did.

When the dishes were wiped and put away, Iris said, "Think I'll turn in. B.J.?"

"You go on, Mama. I'll be up in a minute."

Alone in the chill, dry air of the kitchen, B.J. listened to the air conditioners whine, hugging herself against the cold that ran marrow deep. Aunt Delsey and Ward Trager had a lot in common, she suspected. Unspeakable things had happened to both of them, pulling the linchpin that opened the door to insanity.

From her own experience, she knew that given enough time and stress even the strongest steel, the toughest polystyrene would splinter. A mind worked the same way. Even Mama's with all her avoidance techniques. The question was, where was the breaking point?

The question is, B.J. thought, where is mine?

It had been a tough year. So what? Raising a kid on your own wasn't easy. She never expected it would be. But she had never once considered getting rid of her child. She took the money Chet gave her for an abortion and used it instead to move to Little Rock, away from her mother's shamed tears and constant lectures about how B.J. was ruining her life. A high school drop-out with no skills—still, she managed.

When Denny was small, she worked a night shift assembling telephones and existed on a minimum of sleep. After he was in first grade, she got a job in the school cafeteria and supplemented her income with piecework at home—soldering circuit boards, tying fishing flies, stuffing envelopes. Having to make do and forced to shop in thrift stores, she discovered a talent for repairing things. But people in Little Rock weren't interested in having their toasters repaired. They preferred buying new ones at Wal Mart.

Summers she and Denny would drive north to visit Iris for a couple of weeks. On one of these trips her old Mustang lost a water pump, forcing her to pull off the interstate into a small town, where they were stranded for three days until a replacement arrived. The garage owner's wife felt sorry for B.J., who was planning to sleep in the car with Denny because she couldn't afford the tourist court and offered them a place to stay.

To repay the kindness, B.J. repaired the woman's ancient wringer washing machine. A neighbor asked if B.J. would take a look at her dryer. Word spread, and B.J. found herself with more work than she could handle.

By the following summer, word of mouth added two more towns; soon she and Denny had a regular route. They always made enough to buy gas and food and mail a little extra to a savings account. That money had helped to buy the camper truck and provided a comfortable nest egg.

Then last March B.J. got a cold that turned with frightening speed into bronchial pneumonia, put her in the hospital, and wiped out most of the bank account.

So, yes, she thought now. I've had stress.

More stress than usual. But enough to push her over

the edge into insanity? Well, that depended on the breaking point, didn't it?

B.J. slept badly that night, startled awake several times by nightmares she couldn't remember. The images vanished like primordial monsters sinking quickly beneath choppy water. Finally she gave up, slipped out of bed, and padded downstairs to drink coffee and watch the dawn tint the sky a pale, pearly rose. The only sound was the hum of the air conditioners.

Restless, she remembered the laundry she had left in the dryer the day before and went out to the utility room to fold the clothes.

Shelves lined one side of the tiny room. Up on top was a big U-Haul moving box that contained the odds and ends of B.J.'s childhood, the kinds of things that should be thrown away but never are: old school projects, blurred photographs, keys for locks long forgotten and lost, Brownie pins, letters.

On impulse, B.J. lifted the box down, carried it into the living room, and sat on the floor to look through the contents. Here was her five-year-old handprint preserved in plaster. An aspirin bottle with three desiccated lightning bugs. A picture of B.J. and Iris in front of a Ferris wheel—B.J. with two long fat braids and Iris young and smiling.

Down in the bottom of the box was a yellowed coloring book and a handful of broken crayons. B.J. picked up the blue one, smelled the waxy scent . . . and a faint hint of . . .

. . . cinnamon. Mama was making cinnamon toast, a special treat for B.J.'s third birthday. Mama had bought her a brand-new coloring book and a box of thirty-two Crayolas, a whole rainbow of beautiful colors.

"This is a robin," B.J. said. "But I'm gonna make him blue. Don't you think he should be blue?"

She knew her friend agreed even though she didn't answer—not with regular words, anyway.

64

"Mama's got to work today, but tomorrow we're going to see Mary Poppins. *And then I get to buy something with my quarter that Uncle Dwight gave me for my birthday. Maybe some marbles or an ice cream cone or—"*

"Bethany Jean, you stop that!" Mama grabbed her arm, fingers pinching hard, and jerked her up. "You stop it right now, do you hear me?"

"B.J.? B.J., do you hear me?" Mama's face, but older, hovered over her."

"She was really there," B.J. said.

"What? What in the world are you talking about?"

"It was my birthday. I was coloring and talking to—somebody, then you were yelling, and you spanked me and said you weren't going to have me ending up like Aunt Delsey. Do you remember that, Mama?"

"Oh, B.J., for heaven's sake—" Her mother's eyes shifted, looking away.

"Mama—"

"All this old junk—look at the mess you're making on the rug."

Iris remembered, all right. B.J. was sure of it. But there was no chance to press her because Denny came bounding down the stairs.

"Hey, Mom, what's all this stuff?" he said. "Hey, can I see?"

"No, Denny," Iris said sharply. "I'm starting the pancakes. Put that box away right now and get ready for breakfast."

"Oh, okay." Denny turned to B.J. "Can we look at this later, Mom?"

"Yes," B.J. said, but she was staring at her mother, speaking to her. "Later we will. That's a promise."

11

As Nola backed down the driveway, Frank's old Pontiac pulled up. Shielded by the metal of both automobiles, with four feet of space between them, Nola still found herself leaning away as they passed each other.

Sorry, Bela, the man was a snake, not a vampire. No, what he really reminded her of was a crocodile. She had worked on a movie once that used a whole penful of the loathsome things. Not Florida alligators. Gators weren't pretty, but at least you could stand to look at them without a chill icing your blood. A croc with his warty body and bulging eyes never let you forget that he was mean and vicious and out to tear your leg off if you ventured too close.

I have to get out of that house, Nola thought.

After Frank and Aunt Vee came back from dinner the previous evening, Nola had tried to ease the tension, but quickly gave up and excused herself. She preferred being cooped up in the small guest room rather than endure her aunt's stony silence and Frank's reptilian gaze.

Nola hoped her aunt would mellow; they were blood kin, after all. If Verna had any sense, she would—

eventually—dump Frank, and she and Nola could at least get back to tolerating each other's company.

Meanwhile—a motel, she supposed. There was nothing in Chester. A few run-down places survived in the towns along Route 61, but most of them looked like Norman Bates might come sneaking into the bathroom unannounced. Several chains had motels in Blytheville. She decided to drive there for breakfast and look for a vacancy.

After the jammed freeways and rush-hour gridlock of L.A., she enjoyed the country road with its light traffic. A few puffy clouds floated in the blue rain-washed sky. The air smelled of rich earth, grass, and flowering vetch. And some of those fields of milo and sorghum were hers, she realized. Not that it really mattered, but she wanted to know which ones they were, to park the car and go and walk on the loamy soil.

The sunshine was already warm, but she had dressed in shorts and a white T-shirt jazzed up with screen-printed tropical birds. She drove with the window open. There was no air conditioning in the house on Painter's Island, so she might as well get used to—

Whoa, there, she told herself.

Even though she had thought about staying in Arkansas and living out on the island—well, to tell the truth that was almost all she had thought about last night—she always reached the same conclusion. The idea was at least impractical, probably foolish, and certainly would jeopardize her career. Hollywood had a short memory. Dropping out was easy; trying to get back in might be impossible.

In Blytheville she stopped at the Days Inn along I-55 and booked a room for two nights, hesitated, then inquired about their weekly rate.

You really are nuts, she told herself as she picked up a newspaper and went to find a coffee shop.

Still, after scanning the headlines, she turned to the

classified ads while she sipped orange juice and ate an English muffin. One ad caught her eye. *Let Mr. Fix-It fix it for you. No job too big or too small.* The number had a Chester exchange. After finishing her breakfast, she made the call.

Mr. Fix-It was out, but his wife assured Nola that he had lots of remodeling experience. When the woman heard Nola's name, she asked, "Are you planning to restore that old house on the island?"

Nola was startled; then she smiled. The small-town grapevine still worked as efficiently as the daily paper. "It's just a possibility at this point."

The woman offered to have her husband meet Nola out on the island, but Nola said she would rather have him come by the house in Chester first and discuss the project. They agreed on late afternoon the following day.

Leaving the payphone at the back of the restaurant, Nola caught sight of herself, grinning like a fool, in a mirrored wall in the coffee shop lobby.

My God, she thought, I'm really going to do this. I'm going to move to Painter's Island.

In the car she kicked off her shoes and drove barefoot with the windows open, hair streaming in the breeze, singing along with the most down-home country and western music she could find on the radio, feeling young and happy and free.

She waved to every pickup, every tractor in the fields, to the dour man and his dour gray dog on the porch of the old store beyond the levee.

Stupid to waste money on a motel and have to commute back and forth, she decided. Considering the amount of her savings, she'd have to remodel the house a little at a time anyway. She'd just have to make sure there was always a couple of rooms where she could live and work.

She would have to call the studio later today. And Chuck . . . She didn't necessarily have to end their relationship—it was already on hold while he was off on location. Nola was surprised that she could so calmly consider ending their affair with a phone call.

As she rolled across the pontoon bridge, she saw little effect from the storm. A fallen tree branch, eddies of leaves and twigs in the slough. The weedy yard around the house was still spongy, but there was no sign of flooding. It took more than a summer storm to change the level of the Mississippi. That required acres of winter ice far to the north, melting quickly under a deluge of warm spring rains and sending millions of gallons of water roaring south to gouge out trees, rocks, and tons of soil.

Her great-grandfather had planned well, and built his house on an elevated foundation. Only once had the river rose high enough to enter the building. But, climbing the steps to the narrow front porch, Nola had a sudden clear memory of stepping off that porch into a boat. She remembered Aunt Vee helping her down and then following, her father steering through a vast gray-brown sea, around treetops, past a roof where chickens perched forlornly. The bridge had vanished, along with the boat dock. She had looked back and seen the house, small and isolated, and her grandmother standing there waving.

Grandma stayed, Nola remembered.

"Stubborn as a mule," Daddy had told Mom with a touch of admiration in his voice. "No way to get her out of there unless I hogtied her and threw her in the boat."

Floodwaters never drove Dorothy Douglas from her home. Old age, a weak heart, and crippling arthritis accomplished that. Nola knew she bore a startling resemblance to her grandmother with her oval face and vivid blue eyes. Before it went white, Dorothy's hair had been the same shade of brown that people assumed had been achieved with a henna rinse.

Now if she only had half her grandmother's courage . . .

When Nola opened the door, the inside of the house didn't smell nearly as bad as it had the day before. The airing had helped. Getting rid of the accumulated dust and mouse droppings would improve things too. As she threw open windows, she decided to go back to town later for a broom and a dustpan. Also a mop and a pail—which brought up the question of water supply.

The Mississippi was there at her doorstep, but surely it was too contaminated to drink. Also, there was no power or telephone lines to the island. She thought she remembered a generator. Whether the machine would still work or not . . . this could get complicated, she thought.

But, so what? Walking into the kitchen was like walking into a hug. She stood there for a moment, feeling the warm presence. Maybe this was why Grandma loved this house so much. Maybe Annie had been here for Dorothy, too.

"Looks like it's just you and me, kid," Nola said to the empty room.

With a cross breeze flowing, she looked around for the first time with an eye to what furnishings she could save. Anything valuable had been removed to Chester long ago. Mice and mold had ruined a sofa and the upholstered seats of wooden chairs. But the sturdy tables were fine and so was the writing desk. Even the lamp with the glass pendants could be salvaged with a new shade and some soap and water.

Sound carried a long way out here, so she heard a car coming down the road, and then a *whomp whomp* as it crossed the floating bridge. She went to the window.

Frank's old brown Pontiac pulled into the yard and parked next to her Beretta. Nola assumed Aunt Vee was with him, but then he got out and started toward the house.

Alone.

12

B.J. crouched in front of the big commercial oven, smelling burned grease and charred pie crust. She stared down at the side cutters in her hands as though both the tool and the fingers that held them belonged to somebody else.

The voice was back. And the creep across the back of her neck as the awful, alien feelings and emotions crowded into her skull—

Get out of my head, damn you. Leave me alone.

By concentrating fiercely, she was able to focus on the job. The problem was a short in the wiring. Simple.

She snipped the defective wire and put in a new one. The job was easy, but B.J. felt like she was walking a tightrope while balancing a stack of expensive crystal.

There had been no chance to speak to her mother this morning. Al Norris called after breakfast, saying he needed B.J. to come over right away and get the oven back in service. He offered to rearrange Iris's hours so she could leave just after the dinner rush and spend the evening with B.J. and Denny.

Iris agreed, but B.J. knew she did it because she was afraid to appear ungrateful. Change made her mother tense and jittery. Denny was the only one delighted by the prospect of spending the day at the Crossroads. Despite all their warnings, B.J. knew he had made a beeline for the zoo.

It was broad daylight with people around, and, anyway, B.J. thought Mama's warnings about Ward were exaggerated. Denny would be all right. She wasn't so sure about herself.

She got to her feet, lightheaded, and plotted a careful course to the circuit box, pushed in the breaker, and walked back, one foot in front of the other. Gooseflesh spread like a rash down the length of her spine.

Alien as the touch inside her mind had been, at least the caller had been sending a feeling of happiness. Joy. Not anymore. B.J. recognized the new sensations; she knew them well.

Dread.

Fear.

Foreboding.

Nola could feel Frank's eyes on her as they circled the yard. He trailed her by a few steps, slowing his pace when she slowed hers, keeping his distance. She was very much aware of the way her hips swayed, so she walked stiffly, her buttocks pulled tight. She didn't want to be in the house with him, but it wasn't much better outside.

What she wanted was to tell him to get lost, but the old instincts prevailed. Polite conversation. Civilized interchange. So she babbled on about clearing brush, hauling off the junk in the yard, and about cutting some trees because she wanted a view of the river like the one she remembered from her childhood.

"Sounds like you've been busy," he said.

That flat tone. Since he was behind her, she couldn't see his eyes. They were down by the old storm cellar, wading through knee-high, prickly grass.

I've had enough of this shit, she thought.

"I've still got a lot of things to do," she said. "So if there's something special you wanted—"

She stopped and turned, determined to face him down, to tell him to take a hike if she had to. Caught off-guard, he had no time to shutter the hatred, and it poured from his eyes. No, hatred had been what she got from Aunt Vee. This was malevolence. Pure evil.

Instinctively she took a step back, missed her footing in the hummocky earth hidden beneath the wild grass, and fell.

Sprains, torn ligaments, fractures, casts—all the possibilities flashed through her mind as she went down. Almost all. She never anticipated the movement in the grass. Almost instantly a scaly, slithery body writhed beneath her hand. She glimpsed a wedge-shaped head.

And then the fangs struck, hard and deep.

Pain.

But remote enough so B.J. didn't really feel it. She was doing a good job of keeping the intruder out of her head. Unfortunately, she wasn't doing so well with the oven.

The cook, Jerry, kept a nervous eye on her. No wonder. If she looked half as spooked as she felt, he would be hiding the butcher knives and the meat cleaver.

She tested the wiring with a meter. Everything checked out. Now all she had to do was replace the inside panels and cover the wires.

Ward Trager came in through the back door and spoke to the cook. B.J. couldn't hear what they were saying. Maybe Jerry was warning him off.

Careful. More paranoia.

"Like some help with that?" Ward said.

She realized she'd been standing with the damned panel in her hand, staring stupidly into the oven.

He took one side of the panel and helped her guide it into place. He didn't ask how she was feeling or offer any advice. He just held the metal plate in position while she picked up the screwdriver, positioned the screw, and inserted the thin sharp blade into the slotted groove.

The sky contracted to a bright whiteness. Nola felt the poison arrowing through her veins toward her heart. She screamed. And kept screaming until Frank said, "Jesus, Nola, knock it off."

He stood in front of her with a jagged piece of junkpile wood in one hand, the dead snake in the other. He had chopped the thing's head almost off with the pointed end of the board. The head flopped, hinged by a membrane of green scaly skin. The meat of the body gleamed wetly.

"Wha'—what?" She pressed a thumb as hard as she could into the flesh of her arm above the bite. "What is it?"

"Garden snake." Frank tossed it over into the weeds and stood, looking down at her, holding the board. There was a fresh bloody smear along his shirtsleeve.

She stared at the red holes in her skin. Her stomach roiled, and she tasted bile. "You're sure? Not copperhead —or cottonmouth—or—"

"Believe me," he said. "I know a garden snake when I see one."

Giddy relief mixed with the nausea. She hadn't been poisoned after all. What she was feeling was shock.

She looked up, suddenly aware that Frank had changed positions, but she was staring into the sun and couldn't see clearly, couldn't see his face at all, just saw a blur of motion, and then his body blocked out the sun, and she had one clear image of his rat-sharp features and his hands raising the board and a sunburst of light raying out on the edge of the wood as it swung. . . .

. . . pain struck the side of B.J.'s head, as suddenly and ferociously as a thunderclap. Light splintered against her retinas. She gasped, drawing in air, feeling it locked in her lungs. For one excruciating moment, her whole system shut down.

Then she exhaled in a hoarse whoop and fought for another breath, pain still racing through her head, surprised that she was still upright until she realized that Ward had grabbed her.

"Something—happened—" Her voice sounded thick, slurred.

"The screwdriver slipped," he said.

She thought that was a damned silly thing to say until she realized that blood was running down her arm and dripping from her fingers.

She had been tightening the last screw when the thin blade slid from the grooved head and tore a two-inch gash in her arm, leaving a wound that throbbed and burned.

In spite of the pain, her brain was tracking again, plotting times, and she knew the bright burst in her head had come first, sending a spasm through her body that caused her hand to change the angle of the screwdriver and send the blade skidding.

Something had happened all right. "To *her*," B.J. said. "It happened to her."

She knew she wasn't making any sense, but Ward seemed to understand. Then people were crowding in: the cook, Raylene, Al exclaiming, "oh, Jesus—" in a little puff of beery breath.

B.J. moved back against Ward's hard, lean body, letting him support her, trying to shut out all their voices and listen . . . listen . . .

She had wanted so desperately to have that nagging, whispering intruder gone from her brain, and now she was. There was only cold, dark silence.

13

Frank squatted beside Nola and put two fingers against her jugular. He felt a faint thrumming. She was still alive but barely breathing. He had smacked her a good one with the heavy wood.

A swarm of gnats buzzed around his head. He batted them away, pressed his sweaty face against his sleeve, and sat back in the weeds. He had to think carefully. He had come out here hoping to find Nola—hoping some opportunity would present itself. But what he had done just now was damned stupid. Not his style at all.

What he liked was Dorothy Douglas squirming under her pillow. Or the old widow down in Florida trapped behind the bars on her windows when the fire broke out. Neat and simple. Nola with her skull bashed in—that was a different matter.

Shitty luck, that's what it was. When he heard Nola scream and saw the snake slithering away, he had grabbed the board by instinct and chopped down at the thing with jubilant glee, wondering which variety of poisonous reptile had done his work for him. He was already planning the slow trip to town and the car breaking down. And if she survived the venom, well, there would be plenty of things that could go wrong in the hospital.

Then he picked up the goddamned garden snake and realized his problem hadn't been solved after all. But the thing was, he had seen Nola dead so clearly in his head that he knew by God she ought to *be* dead, so he had just swung the board.

Now he remembered the solid thump as the wood struck her head, the jolt up his arms. He thought about hitting her again using the jagged end. Smashing the nose this time or the cheekbone. Or splitting open the skull like a watermelon.

Blood humming, he flexed his fingers and wiped his palms on his pant legs. Oh, it would be fun all right, but then what? Even some hick county coroner could tell she'd been murdered. All Frank could do to forestall the verdict was to take the body downstream, rent a boat, dump it in the middle of the river, and hope that time and the current would work in his favor.

Not the best idea, though. Way too risky.

Frank swallowed disappointment and stared at Nola. She lay in the long grass with the overgrown, earthen mound of the storm cellar rising behind her. What if she was down here, messing around, Frank thought. It was her property, and she was making plans to stay, so naturally she would want to look things over.

He stood up slowly, grabbed Nola under the arms, and lifted. Grunting, he dragged her a couple of steps and dropped her beside the big wooden cellar door. She was a lot heavier than she looked.

Next he took off his shirt and used the fabric to keep from touching the crosspiece that barred the door, slipping the piece out and pressing Nola's fingers against the wood in all the right places. Still using the shirt and taking care not to smudge his handiwork, he tugged hard on the heavy door.

Rusty hinges creaked slowly open, releasing a puff of cool, damp air that reeked of sour earth and mold. There was no need for a prop. Rust served the purpose, fusing the metal just enough to hold the door ajar.

He considered. Okay. Nola comes out here and opens the storm cellar. Then she gets bitten by the snake, which scares the hell out of her, so she stumbles and falls. Just plain bad luck that she takes a spill into the open cellar.

He looked down into the cavelike opening. There was a sturdy wooden ceiling made of thick, rough boards holding up the earthen mound, a wide bench that ran around three sides and provided a seating and sleeping area, a dirt floor. Trouble was there was nothing to explain the clout on Nola's head.

A quick trip through the yard provided a couple of old rusty paint cans, a few pieces of scrap lumber, and a big old porch swing that leaned against the back of the house. He put everything in the cellar.

Nola went in last, thoughtfully arranged. Frank decided that Nola should snap an ankle in her imaginary fall, so he arranged that, too. When the bone cracked, she cried out once, then passed out again. Her heartbeat was fainter now and her skin a pasty white. Only a matter of time until she was no longer a problem.

He climbed out of the cellar and stood for a moment, staring at the door, reviewing his scenario. Here was poor Nola stumbling into the cellar, breaking an ankle, and banging her head on the swing, and then the door falls shut, trapping her inside. Well, it could happen. Especially after he worked the door up and down once or twice to scrape away some rust. That done, the door fell shut with a nice solid *thump.*

The last thing to be done was to find the dead snake and the board with the telltale bloodstain. He took them across the bridge and walked along the slough to its junction with the river. The water was nice and deep near the old boat dock. He threw in the board and the carcass.

Now all he had to do was to keep Verna from looking

for her niece. He decided to go to the Drop Inn in Chester for a beer and give it some thought.

Ward drove fast toward the clinic in town, keeping an anxious eye on B.J. Her skin was still ashy pale, but she hadn't lost consciousness. The wad of paper toweling she held pressed against the wound was a moist red. The gash was still bleeding, but not badly. It was her eyes that worried him.

They reminded Ward of an FNG in Nam who stepped on a claymore. The FNG—fucking new guy—came and went so quickly Ward did not remember his name, but he remembered the stump of leg spouting bright arterial blood and the thick crimson splatter on the black medic's face and arms as he tightened a tourniquet while Ward held the FNG down.

Most of all he remembered the man's blank, glazed stare, his pupils shrinking to a pinpoint. Looking inward. Or maybe far, far away. Ward heard later that the man died in the Medevac chopper, but not from blood loss. From trauma.

He didn't think B.J. was nearly as deep in shock, still—he glanced at her again and saw that she was shivering. Even though it was hot in Al's old Chevy Luv pickup, he turned on the heater and directed the vent toward her.

"You hold on," he said. "We're almost there."

"'K-k-kay," she said.

He could hear her teeth chattering and cursed himself. Such a big expert on shock and he hadn't thought to bring a blanket.

By the time they arrived at the clinic, he was sweating profusely, but B.J. had stopped shaking and he thought her color was better. Inside, a nurse hustled B.J. off to a curtained cubicle and left Ward to wait in a tiny reception area. He shook his head at a clipboarded questionnaire thrust at him by a clerk. No, he wasn't the husband. He barely knew Ms. Johnson.

He paced around. His sweaty shirt dried quickly in the refrigerated air, leaving him suddenly chilled. He could hear a murmur of voices from the cubicle and smell the sharp odor of Betadyne.

What the hell was he doing here anyway? He had known, as soon as he volunteered, that it was a stupid mistake. Still, what else could he do? Raylene wasn't about to let any of the kitchen help or the waitresses go. As for offering to go herself, fat chance. Iris Johnson insisted that B.J. was all right. A bandage and some hot tea was all she needed until Iris finished her shift and could take her over to the doctor.

Ward told the receptionist that he was going outside for a smoke. A good excuse to escape the waiting room, although he had kicked the nicotine habit long ago with a little help from the Cong. He leaned against the brick facade just outside the clinic door and breathed deeply, warming himself inside and out with the hot, steamy late-afternoon air until the receptionist called him.

A shaken B.J. sat in a chair beside an examining table. She had a little color in her cheeks now and a bandage on her arm.

"Ten stitches," the doctor said, eyeing Ward with careful suspicion. "The arm should be fine, but she's suffering a lot more shock than normal. I'd like to admit her to the hospital overnight, but she refuses to stay."

"I have to get back to work." B.J. stood up, unsteady.

Ward grabbed her arm. "The oven can wait. Come on. I'll take you home."

"She shouldn't be alone," the doctor said.

He gave advice about shock, wrote a prescription for pain pills, and finally released them to deal with the receptionist's demands for immediate payment. Ward told her to bill Al Norris and hustled B.J. out.

In the truck B.J. gave him directions to her mother's house, then sat quietly, cradling her arm.

"Still numb?" he asked.

She nodded.

"You may be in a lot of pain when the local wears off."

He offered to stop and have the prescription filled, but she said she just wanted to get home. He wondered if she had the money for the pills. He would have liked to offer to buy them for her. Being broke had become a way of life, but for the first time in a long while, he found himself wishing for a checkbook or a Visa card.

He was curious about what had caused that screwdriver to slip, but he didn't ask. He sensed the explanation was something dark and strange. Talking about it would forge a connection between them, something he was careful to avoid.

Iris's house was small and unadorned, and the drapes were all tightly closed. Under dense shade the grass was sparse and mowed close to the ground; a spirea hedge was newly clipped. He helped B.J. down from the truck, but she managed the walk to the house on her own.

"You can go on back to work." She fumbled with her key, leaning against the door frame. "I'm fine. Really."

"Sure you are." He took the key, unlocked the door and helped her inside.

The interior of the dark house felt like a meat locker. He put B.J. on the couch, found her a blanket, and readjusted the thermostat. Then he opened the drapes to let in some light and went to put on the teakettle. While the water boiled, he called Al and explained that he would be staying with B.J. for a while.

"Not a good idea," Al said. "I'll send Iris on home."

Catching a glimpse of himself in Iris's shiny toaster, Ward couldn't blame Al for his caution. B.J. was probably afraid of him, too.

When he took the hot tea in to her, he could see she was scared all right. The eyes again. Always in the eyes. He wondered if the fear might come from whatever had happened to her earlier—maybe he wasn't the reason after all.

He told her that her mother would be along soon. "So if you don't need anything else, I think I'll wait for her outside."

"Okay. If you like."

"Well, then—" He stood up, feeling awkward. "Take care of yourself."

"Ward? Thank you," she said.

Outside, waiting for Iris, he told himself he better not get involved. But he couldn't help remembering B.J.'s words there in the restaurant kitchen after the accident. "To *her*," she had said. "Something happened to *her*."

There was a lot more going on here than an accidental slip of a screwdriver. None of his business, though, whatever it was.

Leave it alone, he told himself, good advice that he had every intention of following.

14

Frank wound up having two beers at the Drop Inn because he didn't want to run into Verna, and he remembered that she had a three-thirty appointment to get her hair done. He'd worked up quite a thirst, and the Bud went down smooth, icy cold. He had plenty of time to think things through and come up with the next step.

As soon as he was sure Verna had left the house, he drove over, let himself in, and went up to Nola's room. Moving quickly, he took her suitcases from the closet and stuffed her clothes inside. He thought he might have a problem sorting out her things in the bathroom, but that turned out to be easy. Nola had to be Clinque, shiny silver lids, expensive pale green bottles, fragrance free according to the labels. Verna was Ponds cold cream, Maybelline, and Chantilly bath powder. Even the toothbrushes were a snap. Verna's had to be the old one with the bristles splayed out from use.

Once everything was packed, he took Nola's suitcases down to the basement, hid them behind some old ratty, broken furniture, and draped a blanket over them. No sense raising suspicion by having one of the neighborhood busybodies see him take the bags out to his car. He would get rid of them late some night.

There was nothing left to do but go upstairs, wash the dust off his hands, and wait for Verna.

To pass the time he reviewed the copy of old Dorothy's will, especially the section he had discovered the day before. As Verna had explained to him once, Dorothy had a big grudge against Nola's mother for taking her only grandchild off to California. So the old lady made sure the Douglas money stayed in the family by stipulating that if Nola "died without issue," everything reverted back to Verna.

He decided to have another beer to toast the old gal's foresight. He was polishing it off when Verna arrived. He gave a low wolf whistle.

"Oh, you!" Her cheeks turned pink, and she giggled. "Did Nola ever come back?"

"Came and went," he said.

"Went where?"

"To Memphis, I guess. To the airport. She said she had to get back to L.A."

"Tonight? Without even saying good-bye?"

"You mean she never told you she was going?"

"No. I shouldn't be surprised." Verna sat down and slipped her shoes from her swollen feet. "She's just like her mother. Never thinks of anybody but herself. She didn't happen to mention what her plans are?"

He shook his head. "I suppose I should've asked, but I didn't want her to think I was prying. Maybe I'm just touchy, Verna, but sometimes I get the feeling she doesn't like me very much."

"Well, she better not ever say anything like that to me," Verna said. "I'd never have gotten through all this without you, Frank. Mama—the funeral—"

Her eyes reddened and her mouth trembled. Before the blubbering started, he said quickly, "Now, sweetheart, you know I don't like to see you all upset."

"I'm s-s-sorry. But sometimes I think—what if I lost you? What if you got tired of me and—"

"Well, that's not going to happen, so you just stop worrying about it. You hear me?"

"Okay."

"Good. Now, how about those pork chops you promised me for dinner? I'm starved."

Verna was a terrible cook, but Frank had eaten worse. Over the remains of the coconut cake from the fridge, she got back to Nola. Did he suppose Nola was giving up on her plans to live on Painter's Island? Or was she just going to L.A. to settle things and arrange for a mover?

Frank shrugged and helped himself to another slab of cake. "I suppose we'll know soon enough. Say, isn't it about time for the ball game?"

They finished dessert in front of the TV, watching the Cards skunk the Cubs. Later, after fifteen minutes of Johnny Carson, he kissed her good night, hoping for a quick escape, but she clung to him and begged him to stay.

"Now, Verna, honey, you know how I feel about this. I waited this long to find the right woman, and now I want everything to be perfect for us."

"But I'm tired of waiting. I want you here, please, Frank, and I don't care if we're not married yet."

"Well, I do." He evaded her quivering flesh and moist hands, saying sternly that he was going to be strong for both of them, that he wasn't about to give in to his desires and ruin her reputation.

"It won't be long now," he promised and made a quick exit.

After they were married, he would have to put up with her, at least for a while. He would even have to sleep in the same bed. But not yet. Now he could go back to his room alone and think about Nola dying slowly in the spongy blackness of her prison.

* * *

B.J. lay on the couch, slipping in and out of sleep. She wasn't tired, just gripped by a terrible fatigue. She heard Mama banging around in the kitchen and smelled chicken cooking. Denny tiptoed in, checking on her, then went back to report to Iris.

Earlier B.J. had opened her eyes to find him standing there, staring down, stricken with such vulnerable terror that she managed a smile and said, "Hey, buster, I'm tough stuff. Remember that."

Awake, she tried to recapture the moment just before the accident, but her memory was like some ancient book with its pages crumbling at a touch.

She slept again and dreamed she stood in knee-high grass with the Hendrix's black bull charging toward her. The beast was huge, with red-flecked eyes and great sharp horns atop its massive head. She screamed and ran at him, waving her arms, but he pounded past, so close she felt his rough hide and searing breath, heading straight for the huddled figure that lay behind her in the grass . . .

"B.J.? *B.J.,* wake up." Mama's anxious face hovered above her.

"The bull," B.J. said. "I couldn't stop him. I heard his hooves hitting—"

"It was a bad dream. Probably from those pills the doctor gave you. You just snap out of it now. Sit up and drink some coffee."

Iris made B.J. swing around and put her feet on the floor. The coffee was strong and sweet. After a cupful B.J. felt a little less groggy.

"Where's Denny?" she asked.

"It's ten o'clock," Iris said. "He's in bed. Here, let me get you some more."

This time she brought the coffeepot, filled B.J.'s cup, and put the perculator on a wooden trivet on the end table. Watching her, B.J. was reminded of the women in the little towns along her river route with their soft, unfocused quality.

In Little Rock, B.J. passed the country club on the way

to and from work at Denny's school. She'd see women the same age as her mother, playing tennis or golf, looking youthful and vigorous. They headed up businesses, practiced law and medicine. Her own doctor was one of them. It saddened B.J. that her mother didn't have some of that easy self-confidence.

"I don't think you ought to take any more of that medicine." Iris sat on the sofa next to B.J. and held the saucer while B.J. picked up the cup. "A couple of Advil should do just fine."

B.J. didn't want to tell her mother that she hadn't taken any of the pain pills. The sleepiness wasn't shock —it was related to the voice in her head, the feeling of being watched. She just didn't know how yet. Or she knew how but didn't want to admit it. *Madness?* Some failed genetic trait triggered by God knows what?

"Mama, I have to talk to you," she said.

"Well, I want you to eat something first." She took B.J.'s cup, set it in the saucer, put the saucer on the end table. "I saved you the drumsticks. You used to love drumsticks. Or if you don't want that, I'll open a can of soup—"

"Mama, listen. Please. Something's happening to me. I'm really afraid."

"Oh, B.J., don't be silly. You had a little shock, but you'll be all right. I called the doctor earlier, and he said your arm will be fine."

If Iris had called the doctor, B.J. knew her mother must have been frantic. The worry manifested itself in the way Iris rubbed her hands back and forth, palms down, on the knees of her polyester slacks.

"Ma, I'm not worried about my arm." B.J. put her hand over her mother's to still them. "I didn't take the pain pills. I hear voices in my head. I think I'm going crazy like Aunt Delsey—"

"B.J.—"

"I think I'm flipping out, Ma. Nuts. Wacko. Crackers."

"Oh, B.J., that's—"

"Insane?"

"Ridiculous," her mother snapped. "Anyway, I've told you. Your Great-aunt Delsey wasn't crazy. She just wasn't herself for a while after what happened to the baby."

"That explains Aunt Delsey. What about me?"

Iris pulled away, jumped up, picked up the coffeepot and B.J.'s cup. She fled to the kitchen.

B.J. followed. She felt as though she were wading through water, and her arm hurt with a sudden savage throbbing. She leaned in the doorway and watched her mother turn on the water in the sink and squirt in liquid Joy, filling the room with a soapy, lemony odor.

"Tell me about my birthday, Mama. That day I was three years old. I was coloring. You spanked me and said you weren't going to have me acting like Aunt Delsey."

"Oh, B.J., for heaven's sake." Iris dried the coffeepot, buffing it to a shine. "You went around pretending you had a friend nobody else could see. I guess a lot of kids do that. But I didn't like it. I kept telling you to cut it out, only you wouldn't listen, so I lost my temper and—"

Her voice wavered in and out, overlaid by another fainter voice, calling . . .

B.J. stumbled to a chair and sank down, signaled frantically for her mother to be silent. The connection was weak, like a childhood telephone system of tin cans and baling wire, but there was no mistaking the message. Panic, fear, horror—

"B.J.," Iris said fiercely, "you tell me what you're doing, right now, you hear me?"

"Listening," B.J. said. "Mama, what if you're right and I'm not crazy after all?"

"Well, of course you're not. I told you that."

"Then what I'm hearing is real, Ma. A real person's in terrible trouble, and she's calling out to me for help."

15

mommy, mommy, hurt, afraid I'm so afraid
hold me
rock me
help me

Goddamn wave. She swore she would never body surf
again and here she was diving head first, blackness
rushing up, sand and rock below. Thunderbolts of pain.
Head. Arms. Left ankle. Chest on fire. And nothing she
could do but ride it out, ride the goddamn endless
terrible wave. . . .

mommy, grandma, annie . . . annie . . .

=== 16 ===

I think this is all ridiculous," Iris said. "Hearing people in your head. I bet it's something the doctor gave you, anesthetic, or—"

"Mama, I heard the voice before I went to the doctor," B.J. said. "That was why I hurt myself in the first place."

"Oh, B.J., for heaven's sake. You had an accident. The screwdriver slipped. That's what that Ward Trager said anyway. That *is* what happened, isn't it?" she asked, suddenly suspicious. "It wasn't something *he* did—"

"No, Mama, of course not. Ward was trying to help me. What he told you was true. The screwdriver cut my arm. But the reason it slipped was that I heard her scream—inside my head, Ma—this terrible scream."

"You heard her?" Iris finally stopped fussing around the kitchen and sat down in a chair opposite B.J. "You're talking like this is somebody you know."

"I think it is—maybe—I don't know. She keeps calling for somebody named Annie, so I guess it isn't me, but—"

Iris gasped and sat bolt upright, her face gone milky white.

"Mama? What is it?"

"Annie," Iris whispered. "My God."

"You know who Annie is, don't you? Mama?"

"You," Iris said. "Annie is you."

Nola opened her eyes and cried out. The waves had thrown her on the shore and left her. No—she wasn't on the beach. There was total darkness here, a smell of dank earth and worms and copper. She heard her own heartbeat, not the crash and roll of pounding surf.

Oh God oh Jesus Jesus—dead they think I'm dead and I'm buried—buried alive . . .

But her cheek touched dirt—gritty and cold against her skin. The fetid odor filled her head. If she was in a coffin, there would be a satin lining against her cheek. Nola was a Douglas and Douglases lay on satin in cushioned splendor in Ferman's Funeral Home, surrounded by masses of lilies and tuberoses and carnations.

And caskets were narrow things, the lids inches away. Even though she saw only blackness, she had the feeling of space around her, weighty, oppressive, pinning her down.

If she could feel around and get a fix on something . . . Moving required an absurd amount of concentration and energy, and as soon as she lifted her arm, the pain struck, white hot, icy cold, and centered at the back of her head. The intense burst of agony flared like some kind of interior CAT scan, mapping her skull. She could feel bone shards and the bruised pulp of her brain mass.

Memory rushed back. The snake. Frank. The board swinging. He hit her and left her—but where? The field beside the house? But then there would be open sky, stars, the silhouette of trees. Anyway, if she were in the open, she could be seen, somebody could find her, and Frank was too smart, too cunning behind that crocodile stare. He would hide her—say it. Her body.

If she wasn't dead, she must be dying, hurt so badly he didn't have to worry that she would save herself. She moaned and turned her head slightly, enough to send another jolt of pain temple to temple. She tasted blood, and now she recognized the bright metallic scent mixed in with the odor of fungus and mold.

Pain pulsed, long veins of agony running down her arms, along her spine, rising, falling . . . *Oh, God, help me, somebody, please help me . . .* and then it swept her under.

Iris sat across from B.J. at the kitchen table, shaking her head in disbelief. "You couldn't possibly remember. You were only four months old."

"I don't have to remember," B.J. said. "I hear the damned name, over and over. But I never thought it was me. Why did she call me Annie? Who was she?"

"The little Douglas girl," Iris said. "She couldn't say Bethany, and we didn't use B.J. yet. You were just a baby."

Iris hunched over and crossed her arms, hugging herself. She was still pale, her skin tinged blue from the overhead fluorescents. The whole kitchen seemed leached of color—the birch cabinets and pink walls reduced to dull brown undertones.

"Can't this wait till morning?" Iris asked. "It's late. You need your rest."

"For God's sake, Ma, I slept for hours. Please, I have to know. Tell me about this little girl—"

"Nola. Nola Douglas."

"Tell me about Nola."

The memory wasn't something Iris liked to think about, that much was clear. The story came reluctantly. Iris and Everett Johnson had lived across the river in Arkansas when they were first married. Everett worked at the Air Force Base in Blytheville. Iris wasn't content just to sit home in a little rented cinderblock house. She worked, too, and saved as much money as she could.

There were few decent jobs, and those were hard to get. Iris had no marketable skills because she had dropped out of high school to marry Everett. Another locked compartment there, B.J. sensed. More secrets. She suspected that her parents had a shotgun wedding and that Iris miscarried afterward, although Iris had never even hinted of such a thing. B.J. knew there had been one stillborn baby before she was born.

Now Iris told of working in the hospital in Blytheville, emptying bedpans and scrubbing floors. She picked cotton in the fall, but the big cotton-picking machines were crowding out the day laborers. When she got the job keeping house for the Douglases, it seemed a godsend.

"They had this big old ugly house on an island out in the Mississippi," Iris said. "I can still remember that place. Off in the middle of nowhere. I never could understand why anybody wanted to live there. But it was nice on the inside. I kept it nice. And I liked old Mrs. Douglas. She always treated me right. Her daughter Verna did, too. It was the son and his wife that made all the work. Them and their daughter."

Nola was just a year old when Iris came to work on the island. Getting into everything. She walked at eight months. "Like a little tornado," Iris said. "And spoiled rotten. Her mother just let her run wild. Her grandmother wasn't quite so bad, but the little girl was already the spitting image of Mrs. Douglas, so naturally she had a soft spot for the child. She'd drop everything to sit in the kitchen and rock her to sleep."

Then Iris had gotten pregnant. By that time, they had some money saved. Because of losing her last child, she planned to quit as soon as she started to show, but disaster struck. Everett lost his job at the base. It was winter, and there was no farm work available.

"That's when your daddy's migraines started," Iris said. "Some days he couldn't even get out of bed they were so bad. I was lucky Mrs. Douglas let me stay on. But it was hard that last month with me worrying about you, and that Nola—Lord, she ran me ragged. She was always putting her hands on my belly to feel you move. Her mother told her I had a baby inside, not that a child that age had any business knowing such things."

Iris worked until she went into labor, and then she went back when B.J. was two weeks old.

"I couldn't depend on your daddy to watch you, not with his headaches, so Mrs. Douglas found me this big old willow basket for you to sleep in. You were healthy, thank the Lord, and so good, you hardly ever cried."

Everything would have been fine except that Nola wouldn't leave the baby alone. She was constantly hugging and kissing B.J. "One day I came into the kitchen and found her all stuffed inside that basket with you, sound asleep. Scared me to death, I can tell you. I thought for sure she'd smothered you.

"She needed a good spanking, but nobody ever touched her. I think old Mrs. Douglas was beginning to see she was out of hand, and I'm sure Verna would've liked to take a switch to her, but Faye would have a fit if anybody so much as raised their voice to the little brat.

"It got so I hardly got any work done because she wouldn't leave you alone. She'd bring you bugs and leaves and rocks. And she was forever trying to share her food, stuffing pretzels and cookies in your mouth."

That last day Iris had been trying to finish the vacuuming while Nola took her nap. When she came back to the kitchen, she found Nola there, sitting in the rocking chair with B.J., smiling, delighted with herself.

"How she got you up in that chair I'll never know. She could've dropped you—killed you. Well, I snatched you away and walloped her so hard. She screamed bloody murder, and you started crying. Faye came storming in. She wouldn't listen when I tried to tell her why I hit the child. She just ordered me out of the house. I thought Mrs. Douglas would stick up for me, but she didn't," Iris said bitterly. Even after all these years the memory clearly rankled.

"The worst part was Faye told everybody how I beat

up her little kid. People acted like I was a criminal. I was glad when your daddy wanted to leave and come over to Tennessee to look for work."

"So you never saw the Douglases again?" B.J. asked.

"Not after we left Arkansas."

B.J. could imagine Nola growing more and more attached to the little baby in the willow basket. In a strange way she could almost remember the way the child had felt.

"She loved me," B.J. said.

Iris looked surprised, but she nodded. "I suppose she did. I ran into Verna one day just before we moved. She said that Nola just about drove them crazy carrying on and crying for you."

"It must be her, Mama. She must be the one who's calling to me."

"Oh, B.J., I can't believe it. Nola was just a baby herself. Even if such a thing was possible, and I'm not saying it is, I doubt she'd even remember you. It just doesn't make sense."

"I know it doesn't."

"Well, then, if you ask me, I think you ought to put it right out of your head. Forget it." Iris stood up, pushed in her chair. "Lord, it's almost midnight. Come on, B.J. We better get to bed."

"I'm going to stay up for a while. You go ahead."

"And leave you down here alone?"

"I'm all right. She's—she's gone, for now."

"Are you sure?"

"I'm sure."

"Well, don't stay out here in the kitchen. Go sit on the couch. I'll leave my door open, and you holler up if you need me."

B.J. promised she would and, on impulse, hugged her mother before she went upstairs, surprising them both.

Alone, in the quiet living room, B.J. leaned back and closed her eyes. Was it really possible? She could almost see that shadowy little girl, leaning down, chattering nonsense. It was as though her mother's words had touched some hidden recess of her mind and revived old, forgotten images.

What if something strange—something impossible—had taken place, some bonding forged between the two of them that went far beyond the realm of the ordinary? Her friend when she was a child, the other little girl that nobody else could see—was that Nola, too? And why had the connection been broken?

No—why had the connection been reestablished again? That was the question that really needed an answer.

She got up and went out to the kitchen, wobbly but tracking a little better. It was difficult to use the telephone with one hand. She cupped the receiver between her ear and her shoulder while she dialed.

Information in Chester, Arkansas, had no listing for Nola Douglas, but there was one for Verna. Awkwardly juggling the phone, B.J. wrote the number down. She looked up at Mama's big round kitchen clock. 12:45. Much too late to call. She should wait until morning.

She dialed anyway. After three rings a sleepy voice said hello.

"I'm sorry, I know it's late," B.J. said, "but I'm looking for Nola Douglas."

"Nola? She went home."

"But she was there?"

"She came for the funeral," the woman said. "But she left."

"There was a funeral? I'm sorry. Who—?"

"My mother."

"You're sure Nola left?"

"Well, of course. I told you, she went back to L.A."

"Can you give me her phone number please? I really need to speak to her."

"It's the middle of the night," the woman said irritably. "I'd have to go downstairs and look it up—who is this anyway?"

"Just a friend. Is she in the telephone book? I'll be glad to ask information for the number."

"You do that."

Click.

Probably Nola's aunt Verna, B.J. thought. She had a right to be upset, being awakened from a sound sleep. She sounded sure enough that Nola had gone home. After the funeral—Verna's mother's, Nola's grandmother's funeral. Could that be all that had happened? Had it simply been Nola's grief that B.J. felt?

Nola was probably very close to her grandmother. B.J. remembered Iris telling how much the little girl looked like Dorothy Douglas, how fond the woman was of Nola.

Nola might be grieving still, but safe at home in Los Angeles, in no danger at all. There was one way to find out. B.J. called information. A long shot—a huge place like L.A., there must be hundreds of people named Douglas—but she got lucky. There was only one named Nola. A disembodied voice reeled off the number.

Shaky now, she pulled over a chair and sat down before she dialed again. What the hell am I going to say? she thought, panicked. Hi, this is your infant playmate. I just wondered if you were calling me up on the ESP hotline—

In L.A. Nola's phone rang. A click, silence, then a bright voice repeated back the number and added, "Chuck and I aren't here right now, but if you leave your number . . ."

B.J. sat with the cold, blue-white light of the kitchen fluorescents pouring down, a chill of recognition snaking along her spine. She realized that a beep had sounded and that the rush of sound on the line must be the tape of an answering machine. She hung up.

There could be a dozen reasons why Nola had not answered the phone. She might routinely screen her calls.

She might be out on the town, dinner and dancing at one of the places B.J. read about in *People* magazine.

B.J. wished—God, how she wished—this was true. But she knew it wasn't. Nola was calling her. And it wasn't grief that rang through her head the day before. It was a cry of pure terror.

17

I have to do something, B.J. thought. But what? Get into her truck and drive to Chester? Her pickup was still at the Crossroads, left there after the accident.

Her mother's car? Forget it. Iris would have a fit. B.J. wouldn't be surprised if her mother physically prevented her from leaving. And the way she was feeling, that wouldn't be hard to do. Her strength was draining away at an alarming rate.

At least she should call Nola's aunt and tell her— what? When B.J. thought about the energy required to actually convince Verna that something might be wrong, she knew she couldn't do it.

She didn't have much choice. She would have to rest tonight and try to find Nola tomorrow.

Ward opened his eyes in the darkness and he was instantly awake. After six months on patrol you learned to hear not just with your eyes, but with your skin, your nose, your balls. Jungle radar. You either developed it or you woke up to find your throat slit, a great wide second mouth spilling blood.

Seventeen years now since he had spent his nights in that edgy twilight state that passed for sleep. Most of the time he rested well. But occasionally something would trigger the old instinct, and his body would go back on jungle alert.

He saw motion in the wolf run. Lobo had come out of the cage. The wolf paced back and forth in a mad lope. Ward didn't so much hear the paws on the soft dirt as feel the *slap-slap* vibrating through the ground. He wondered if the animal had eaten any of the muskrat. He knew some of the carcass was left. He could smell the rank odor of the meat.

On the other side of the fence Ebbie moved around nervously, ears pricked toward the run. Guess we're both spooked, Ward thought, shifting restlessly on the hard ground.

Spooked, like B.J. Yes, that described the way she was acting before the accident. It was more than that afterward, of course. And now? Al had called Iris before closing to check on B.J. Ward put the idea in his head. Al had been sucking up the beer and was too soused to think of it on his own. Iris told Al her daughter was just fine, which was what Ward hoped to hear, but the reassurance didn't ease his mind.

No point in worrying about her. It was out of his hands. He decided not to think about her anymore. He could do that if he tried, zero things out completely. A trick of survival learned in the POW camp.

He could do it with B.J. The wolf was a different matter.

slap-slap
slap-slap

He kept falling asleep, only to be startled awake by the sound that resonated through the earth, penetrating his bones. Once he sat up and called out, "Remy?"

His heart knocked dryly, and there was a moment when he knew that if he looked over at the run, Remy would be there, pacing, pacing.

I need a drink, he thought. He kept a bottle of cheap bourbon in his pack. But if he started now, he'd be dead drunk by morning. Raylene would put up with that from Al, but not from him.

He forced himself to look at the run lit only by starshine. This time it was the dream that awakened him, not the wolf. The run was empty.

It didn't matter, though, once the radar was on. Jungle sleep.

At dawn, fighting the buzzy headache of exhaustion, he thought he might as well have given in to his urge for the damned bourbon.

The distant whine of the vacuum cleaner awakened B.J. She knew it was late. Morning sunlight lit the closed blinds with a fierce glow. Her little travel alarm read: 10:35.

The night before, after an hour in bed, the pain in her arm had flared with such intensity that she had gratefully swallowed a codeine and Tylenol pill. Now her brain felt heavy, foggy, full of a dim urgency that she couldn't quite place. Then she remembered. Mama's story, the phone calls, Nola's voice . . . She fumbled out of bed. The motion put pressure on her injured arm, so that she yelped with pain.

Denny came rushing in. "Mom? What is it? What happened? Are you all right?"

"I bumped myself, honey. I'm okay."

"Are you sure? Should I get Grandma?"

His face was pale and tense, his eyes huge with fright. She was suddenly sure he had come several times to stare down at her while she slept.

"Hey, worrywort, lighten up. I just had a little accident, that's all."

B.J. could hear the falseness in her voice and knew he heard it, too. Oh, God, she was as bad as Mama, keeping secrets.

She could easily have made it alone, but she said,

"Would you help me into the bathroom? I'm still a little groggy from the medicine."

"Sure."

He put his arm around her waist, offering his small, sturdy body for support, happy to be useful. He walked with her, then said he would wait right by the door in case she needed him.

By the time she finished, her mother had joined Denny in the hall. Both faces watched her uneasily. She let Denny lead her downstairs while Iris hurried on ahead to heat up the coffee.

In the kitchen B.J. shook her head to Mama's offer of scrambled eggs and bacon. "What I could eat is a doughnut."

"A doughnut? For heaven's sake, B.J., you need some nourishment, not—" Iris broke off, reading B.J.'s glance at Denny. "Well, if that's what you want, maybe Denny could run over to the Stop and Shop."

Denny went reluctantly, wearing that accusing gaze that let B.J. know he wasn't fooled for a minute. He knew she was trying to get rid of him.

After he raced away on his skateboard, B.J. told Iris about the phone calls to Verna and to Nola's number out in L.A. But, sitting there at her mother's old Formica table with the sunlight streaming in, she felt her conviction slipping. Echoing the ambiguity, Iris kept shaking her head in disbelief.

"I should never have told you all that old stuff about Nola Douglas," Iris said. "You just let your imagination run wild."

"Maybe, Ma. I don't know. Last night—hearing her voice on the phone—I was so sure—"

"Last night you were hurt and upset and shot full of God knows what-all kind of medicine," Iris said firmly. "Anyway, if Nola is anything like she was when she was little, she can take care of herself."

"But what if she really is in trouble? I should at least call her aunt and tell her my suspicions."

"You'll do no such thing," Iris said, aghast. "My daughter, after all these years, calling up with a story like that—she'd think I put you up to it—for spite—or to pay them back—or—"

"All right, Mama. Okay. I won't call."

B.J. wasn't ready to concede that her mother was right, but she didn't want to argue. The pain in her arm had quieted to a dull throb. Her head hurt, an ache brought on by hunger. She would have loved the bacon and eggs her mother had offered earlier, but now it was a point of honor to wait for the damned doughnuts.

"You'll see," Iris said. "You rest today and put this out of your mind. By tomorrow you'll be glad I talked you out of calling Verna."

She was probably right. At the very least, B.J. knew she shouldn't go off half-cocked. Give it some time. Maybe she would even try Nola's number in L.A. again. Meanwhile—

She heard the skateboard swoop into the driveway. Denny charged through the back door, filling the kitchen with his energy. B.J. decided she must be looking more normal because he eyed her with relief and launched into a nonstop report on yesterday's activities at the petting zoo while she devoured the jelly-filled Hostess O's with their thick coating of powdered sugar.

She listened and nodded in all the right places, but all the while a little spark of foreboding jumped around in the back of her head. Although she had a solid core of her mother's common sense, she also knew not everything in the world depended on logic and reason.

Waiting might be the logical thing to do or it might just as easily be wrong, very wrong. How to tell the difference?

Only Nola would know.

18

Ward took a break at midmorning, locked the gate to the zoo, and left the sign that read: BACK IN TEN MINUTES. His head still ached from lack of sleep, and he badly needed a cup of coffee. The sun dazzled off the asphalt and the glass and chrome of vehicles in the parking lot. B.J.'s truck sat over in the corner, looking abandoned.

Entering the back door of the Crossroads' kitchen was like walking into the heat of a steel mill. Earlier, Ward had finished installing the door panel on the oven B.J. had worked on yesterday. The repair job was a success because both ovens were going full blast, the hot air redolent of apples and cinnamon.

Standing at a butcher-block worktable, Jerry muttered to himself as he flattened pie crusts with a steady *whap-whap* of the rolling pin. His face shone with sweat, and there were big wet blotches on his shirt.

"A pisser," he said balefully.

Figuring he meant life as a whole, Ward said, "Sure is," and went on through the swinging door. He poured himself some coffee, took the mug in, and sat down on the first stool at the end of the counter. Raylene was up front running the cash register, but she homed in on him instantly.

He saw her reach for the account book she kept on a shelf beneath the register, making a big deal of pointedly observing his drink and marking the entry. His pay was a percentage of the ticket sales for the zoo. From that she deducted everything he ate and drank in the restaurant. He kept no record himself, but he suspected she cheated him. Not much—a nickel here, a dime there. He really didn't give a shit. Or he hadn't until yesterday.

The memory still rankled—the contempt in the clinic receptionist's eyes as she sized him up for a deadbeat. His urge to help B.J. and the frustration of knowing there was damned little he could do, especially without money.

Al might have phoned to find out how B.J. was doing, but Al wasn't in yet, which meant he must have continued his binge last night after closing. Ward doubted Raylene would care enough to have called Iris.

He could call himself. At least he had enough money for that. Or he might go for supplies and make a casual stop at Iris's house. But that meant clearing the errand with Raylene so he could use the truck and close the zoo. He knew she'd never agree.

Raylene brought two truckers to a back booth, seated them, and detoured over by Ward to say, "Your account is getting close to breaking even, and you know how I feel about feeding you on credit. You better have some customers today."

She stalked away before he could reply. What the hell did she expect him to do, put up a roadblock and snag people off the highway? Probably. He drained his coffee and went back outside.

Under the metal roof of the zoo enclosure, the rattlers lay in torpid coils. As he cleaned up sheep dung, he could hear the wolf's heavy panting.

Ward had finally thrown away the remains of the muskrat. This morning's beef lay untouched in the run,

105

drawing flies. After a night of ceaseless pacing, the wolf lay unmoving in the cage and watched Ward with pale, glassy eyes. The animal's body looked skeletal under the dull pelt. The starvation was slow and painful, but Lobo didn't have the willpower to stop eating entirely.

So what am I supposed to do? Ward thought.

What he ought to do was bundle up the sleeping bag and start walking. Hitch a ride. Where? North? West? He had lived beside isolated Minnesota lakes with only loons for company. He had spent two years in the highest, loneliest reaches of the Rockies, wintering once in a lean-to he had turned into an ice cave, and once in an abandoned silver-mining town with a relentless wind howling down from icy peaks. There were always places to go, if he wanted to leave.

An Indiana car pulled in and parked. A pit stop, Ward thought, but the three kids were pointing and begging, look, Mom, can we—I wanna—please, Daddy. They came back from the Crossroads with tickets.

Enough for a light lunch, Ward decided. He wasn't as good at ignoring the hunger pangs as he used to be. Just as the family left, Iris's Dodge arrived. Denny jumped out of the back, waved and called, "Hey, Mr. Trager." The boy opened the door on the passenger side for his mother.

Ward left the enclosure and angled over. Iris glowered, then ignored him to say to B.J., "Now, you be careful driving back. Pull off the road if you—" She paused. "If you have to. And don't take any more of those pills."

"Okay, Ma." B.J. turned to smile at Ward and say hello. She looked weary, and she cradled her injured arm against her body, but her face had lost most of that dazed confusion.

"You take care of your mother," Iris said to Denny, but she never took her eyes off Ward, measuring his proximity to her daughter. "And don't go bringing that skateboard into my kitchen."

Iris didn't want to leave, but she did, glancing nervously at her watch. She was ten minutes early for her shift, but to Iris that was late.

"How's ole Lobo today, Mr. Trager?" Denny asked. "Did he eat anything?"

"Not much," Ward said.

"Can I go see him? Is it okay, Mom?"

"Well, maybe for a minute." Denny was off like a shot, so B.J. had to yell, "Watch for cars!" She looked up at Ward. "I hope that was all right with you. It's not easy to say no to him."

"I noticed that," he said. "It's fine, he's a good kid." An awkward pause. He knew what he wanted to say, but he felt as though his speech center was rusty from disuse. "I'm surprised you came here. I mean, I didn't think you'd feel like going out."

"I didn't want to leave the truck."

She began walking over toward the Toyota, tracking okay, he saw. He trailed along. The asphalt was soft underfoot, giving off a hot, tarry smell. B.J. wore a jeans skirt and a red tank top with the neck cut low, revealing the swell of her breasts. She carried her purse slung over her shoulder. Stopping beside the pickup, she fumbled with her keys, tried to insert them into the lock, and dropped them.

"Damn," she said, kneeling.

"Here." Reaching for the keys, his fingers closed over hers—and stayed for a ridiculously long moment while he noticed the fine sheen of sweat on the tops of her breasts and a pulse beating in her throat. He felt something physical jump between them, almost a static charge.

She glanced up, startled. He quickly got to his feet and looked away, not wanting to see the next expression—fear, disgust, whatever it was sure to be—leap into her eyes. He opened the door and handed the keys back to her.

"Gotta go," he mumbled. "I'll send Denny over."

"Thanks, and thanks for yesterday."

"No problem."

Asshole, he told himself as he hurried off toward the zoo. What the fuck's your problem?

Jesus, you'd think he had been a monk these past years. But this was different. He was different with her. There were engines inside him, long silent, turning over, throbbing to life. He wasn't altogether sure he liked the feeling.

B.J. leaned against the pickup and watched Ward walk away. A strange man. He was skittish as the animals he tended. Mama thought he was dangerous. Maybe so. But he was gentle, too, and protective. She had seen that side of him yesterday. And now there was a sexual spark between them to muddle her thinking some more.

She could do without another complication. God knows she had plenty. Mama's pressure to sweep every-thing under the rug, to pretend she didn't see it so maybe it would go away. Denny's worry and the erosion of their closeness.

And Nola . . . B.J. still couldn't shake the feeling that something was terribly wrong there.

Across the parking lot she saw Ward speak to Denny, then Denny came running toward her. Standing beside the truck, she managed to roll down the window, sat on the front seat, swung her legs inside, and considered how she would close the door. The vinyl burned her fanny through her skirt and back.

When Denny came charging up, she said, "Shut the door for me, would you?"

He did, then started around the truck.

Denny?"

"Yeah, Mom?" He stopped, came back.

"How would you like to stay and help Mr. Trager for a while? I know it's boring for you just hanging around with me, and you really don't have to. All I'm going to do is go back to Grandma's and take a nap."

"Are you sure, Mom?" He looked worried, torn between wanting to stay and feeling that he should go with her. "You won't pass out or anything?"

"Nope. I'll be fine. I'll come back for you later, okay?"

"Okay. Thanks, Mom." He ran off, waving good-bye.

Driving with one hand was difficult but not impossible. She kept her promise to Denny to stay conscious. She only heard the whispers once in a while, and they were so faint, the low voltage didn't have enough power to shock her into careening off the road.

Back in her mother's quiet house, B.J. lay on the couch, closed her eyes tightly, and strained to tune in, to listen with her mind. All this time she had resisted the voice in her head. Now that she was prepared to hear it, now that she wanted the damned thing to be there—nothing.

It occurred to her, lying there, that maybe this wasn't just a one-way transmission. Maybe she could send as well as receive. Was it possible?

Nola—whoever you are—wake up. Wake up and talk to me.

Of course she still didn't know for sure it *was* Nola. She finally got up and went to call Nola's number in L.A. again. If Nola answered, she might even tell her the whole silly story, give her a good laugh. If she answered.

B.J. called and got the machine. Hearing Nola's voice, a gelid rash of gooseflesh prickled the back of her neck.

It *was* Nola who called to her. She knew it this time with desperate certainty. B.J. went back to lie on the couch.

Nola, damn you, Nola, where are you?

She imagined she was yelling to Denny when he was two, that day he had pulled out of her hand to run toward the busy street, and she had commanded him with the force of her voice to stay out of traffic. She just reached right out with her voice to jerk him to a stop on the curb.

Nola, you answer me. Answer me right now. Nola! NOLA!

No response.

Nothing.

══ **19** ══

Nola, you answer me right now, young lady. Do you hear me?

"Grandma?" Nola's eyes flew open.

She had taken her sand pail and shovel and sneaked away to play down by the river. She wanted to build a sand castle, but Mommy had said no, and so had Grandma. Too close to naptime, they said, but she went anyway.

Water lapped on her bare feet. The sun was honey warm on her head. Her eyes drooped close, and then the day had just slipped away. She must have fallen asleep there on the river bank. Now her grandmother was calling, a raw edge of panic in her voice.

It was so dark—had she slept all afternoon and evening? No, this wasn't a nighttime darkness. She wasn't beside the river at all. She was inside some small, enclosed place. A slit of light traced a rectangle overhead. A door.

The storm cellar door. She was in the cellar, but it looked different, full of strange, angular shapes. What was she doing down here? She didn't remember coming,

111

but she didn't always. Sometimes Daddy picked her up out of her bed and brought her here when the weather got so bad they thought for sure a tornado would drop down from the clouds. Then she'd wake up and see them all there, sitting on the benches, faces yellow in the glow of the lantern hanging from the planked ceiling.

Where was everybody? Why was she all alone? She tried to sit up, but fingers of pain clamped her neck and held her down. The cellar swayed around her as though it had come loose from the ground to float—float, yes, of course, she remembered now.

Rain, a storm. Daddy leaving in a boat, steering in among the trees. A panther crouched atop a barn. Why had Daddy left her here all by herself?

"Daddy, please come back," she whispered. "Please, I wanna go home."

But he didn't come and neither did Mommy or Grandma. Nobody came.

"Daddy, Mommy!" Her scream came out a harsh croaking. Her tongue was swollen and her throat was horribly dry. They would never hear. She was lost. Lost forever. There was only one person who always heard when she called. There was always Annie.

Frank walked along the river's edge, carrying a fishing pole, wearing a pair of waders. If anybody saw him, well, there was nothing remarkable about a man looking for a few catfish for dinner.

He hadn't wanted to drive out to the island. Nobody would probably notice, but why take the chance? So he had parked up by the old ferry landing and headed south on foot.

Here and there along the sandy shore grew stands of scrubby willow, but mostly the vegetation ran to rank weeds as high as his head intertwined with fat May pop vines, bearing huge purple flowers that smelled like decaying flesh.

When the plants grew right down into the water, he

could wade around without getting his feet wet. The high boots protected him from snakes, too, an added bonus.

It was past noon, so mostly he was shaded by the foliage. Even so, it was a hot, steamy walk. By the time he reached the pontoon bridge, he was sweating steadily and wishing for a cold beer.

He could have saved himself a lot of trouble if he had hit Nola a little harder. A pain in the ass, but he had to check on her. You couldn't be too careful with these things.

He reached for the canteen of water he'd brought along strapped to his belt. Took a swallow and made a face. The stuff tasted like dog piss, but at least it was wet. He bet old Nola would've liked some along about now.

As he walked, he kept an eye out just in case she had somehow managed to get out of the cellar. The door was barred so her escape was probably impossible. The thing he really had to worry about was somebody letting her out. Of course, that was the kind of news that would be announced by the cops, and since they hadn't come calling . . .

Frank noticed a glint off the chrome of Nola's Beretta in the trees where he had hidden it. Still there. He was pretty sure this was all a big waste of time.

Ahead the ugly old house crouched in the weedy yard. Deserted. Everything looking just the way he had left it. With Nola out of the picture, it might not be a bad idea to talk Verna into moving out here. The place had a lot more possibilities than the house in Chester. Wiring chewed by rats, unheated rooms requiring space heaters, fireplaces—the thoughts all followed a similar vein. A natural since he had some experience along these lines. The building must be tinder dry, and it was a hell of a long way to the nearest fire department.

Savoring the plans, he headed for the storm cellar, noting with satisfaction that the door was still closed and barred. He took out his handkerchief and opened it, saying "knock knock."

Nola was inside all right, lying on the dirt floor. Not dead. No such luck. She threw her hand up against the brightness of the sun, making a mewling sound like a maimed cat.

She said something, too, the words thick and slurred. He thought she called him Daddy.

"Crap," he said and slammed down the door.

He took another swig of water and wished he had hit her again yesterday. He really ought to go ahead and do it now. But murder was one thing. Getting away with it was quite something else.

On the up side, she hadn't gotten out of the cellar. Matter of fact, he'd swear she was still lying pretty much the way he'd left her. And she looked as though she couldn't possibly last much longer.

Still, it bothered him as he left the island and crossed back over the bridge. Too many things could go wrong until she was safely buried beside old Dorothy over in Mt. Zion Cemetery.

Verna called L.A. early that morning, fuming about her niece taking off without revealing her plans. Getting Nola's answering machine just made Verna madder. Frank knew Verna would not quit trying to reach Nola until she had a chance to bawl her out.

Eventually Verna would realize something was wrong. *When* she realized it was the key. Everything always came down to timing.

Working his way back to the river along the slough, he saw a ripple in the muddy water, and at the V of the wake a dark brown snake moved in an S-shaped crawl. It was olive brown with darker crossbars. Water moccasin. Big bugger. Lots of people couldn't tell the difference between water moccasins and other water snakes. Frank always could.

If he moved quickly, he could jump in the water and grab the thing. He knew just the way to do it, how to latch on right behind the head with one hand and get a good hold of the body with the other.

When he was fourteen, he had spent a year with his uncle Toover, who used snakes in his revival meetings and expected his nephew to earn his keep by taking care of the reptiles. These snakes had not had their venom sacs removed, either. Uncle Toover wanted the real thing to flaunt the power of God.

So Frank could do it all right. He could catch the water moccasin, take it back to the storm cellar, and see how long Nola would last with some real poison flowing through her veins.

But what about Joe Blow Coroner? What would he think? Two snake bites. One poisonous, one not. What were the chances of that happening? Of course, if Nola was in that cellar long enough, maybe nobody would notice. There were rats, other scavengers . . .

The water moccasin still hadn't noticed him. It moved right next to Frank in the water, curving lazily toward him. A little insurance. What could it hurt?

20

Mr. Trager, do you think maybe you oughta take Lobo to the vet?" Denny stood in front of the cage where the wolf lay listless and panting heavily in the heat.

"I don't think I can do that," Ward said.

"Why not?"

"Well, in the first place, he's not my animal. I don't think the Norrises would agree to have him treated. Vet bills can run pretty high."

Denny nodded soberly. He understood the constraints of not having money. "Well, maybe he'd like something different to eat. Some french fries or a hot dog."

Ward knew a change of diet wasn't going to help the wolf. The animal's eyes followed him everywhere now. That familiar, imploring stare—Remy's stare.

He didn't want to tell Denny he thought the wolf had gone insane, so he said, "Could be. I guess a few french fries couldn't hurt."

Denny promised to bring part of his lunch to Lobo, then got busy cleaning the enclosure, filling water troughs, and scattering corn for the chickens.

Until he began working at the Crossroads zoo, Ward never thought about kids much. They simply were not part of his life. But from brief contacts in rest areas and restaurants along the interstate, he found he liked their frank curiosity a lot better than their parents' hostility. Daily observation at the zoo hadn't made him suddenly love the little tykes, but seeing them in action made him realize they were just people, only shorter, who had not yet learned the social niceties of covering up their feelings.

Nothing, however, had prepared him for Denny Johnson. The boy had a steady, clear-eyed sweetness that immediately sank a hook into Ward's heart. He had overheard and observed enough to know what B.J.'s and Denny's life must be like. A gutsy lady, raising a child on her own.

He kept thinking about that moment in the parking lot with B.J. Jesus, like some old corny fifties movie. He remembered the sheen on her skin from the sun and the swell of her breasts. He wondered if she had a boyfriend back in Little Rock—a lover. He thought it would be easy to pump Denny for the information, then immediately felt ashamed of the impulse. He tried putting her out of his mind like he had the night before, but it wasn't so easy this time.

One or two tourist families straggled in. The kids were docile enough. The heat seemed to tone down their aggressiveness. In between customers Denny talked about the towns he and his mother visited during the summer. "We ought to be in Watson. Or maybe Marvell. Usually we don't come to see Grandma this soon."

A worried shadow crossed his face. Ward thought the boy would have said more, but just then a car drove up, and Denny ran off to keep an eye on Ebbie.

Around noon Al Norris pulled into the parking lot, bleary-eyed, and waved to them. "Hot work there, you two," he yelled over.

A few minutes later a busboy brought two take-out containers of Pepsi from the kitchen.

Ward and Denny sat in the shade of the overhang,

sipping the cold drinks. Denny twirled his straw in the ice, studying it for a while before he finally said, "Mr. Trager? You were there when my mom cut her arm, weren't you?"

Ward nodded.

"Well, was it really bad? Did she hurt herself some other way?"

"What do you mean?"

"Did she fall down and bump her head or something?"

"No," Ward said. "She didn't fall. And the cut wasn't very deep. A few stitches, that's all."

Denny was a smart kid, so of course he suspected there was more to it than just an accident with the screwdriver. But since Ward didn't understand what caused the shock or the look in B.J.'s eyes, he certainly wasn't going to tell the boy about those things and alarm him even more.

"My friend, Jody, cut his leg on this piece of metal last fall," Denny said. "He got nineteen stitches. It hurt a lot, but he didn't act like Mom did. Him and me played Nintendo that night."

"Some people just react differently, I guess."

"What about when you hurt yourself?"

Ward stared at the ridges of scar tissue running across the backs of his hands, crossing the palms in a grotesque mockery of life lines.

"What about it?"

"Well, do you remember how you acted when it happened?"

Ward remembered . . .

The grin on the Cong's face as he tied Ward's wrists, the knife, bright hot pain and the blood. How he ground his teeth against the screams. Later, in the cage, he wept with relief because the cuts were shallow, and no tendons had been severed. Then the infection set in. Angry red, pus white, swollen, the skin so stretched and painful— when he finally couldn't stand it any longer, he remembered how he had wrung his hands together to break the pus sacs. . . .

"What happened to me was nothing like what happened to your mother," Ward said harshly.

He stood up and went to pitch his empty paper cup into a trash barrel. Denny scrambled to his feet and followed along behind him.

"I'm sorry, Mr. Trager. Mom says sometimes I don't know when to keep my big mouth shut."

Ward looked down at the earnest, contrite face. How did you stay mad at this kid? "It's okay, Denny. There are just things I'd rather not talk about."

"Okay. That's cool." A long pause, then, "Mr. Trager? Yesterday—the doctor didn't say anything, did he? About my mom? Like she has something else wrong with her?"

"No, Denny. Nothing like that. Hey—" Ward patted him awkwardly, feeling the bony wings of his shoulderblades. "Your mom's going to be okay."

"I hope so. It's just me and her, you know? I don't have a dad. Well, I mean I do, everybody's got a dad, but mine didn't want me or Mom, so—"

He broke off and turned away, but not before Ward saw the shine of tears in his eyes. Denny went to stand and stare at the wolf. Ward followed him, wishing he knew what to say to ease the boy's mind.

"It's not right the way he just lays there," Denny said, gazing at Lobo. "I liked him better all mean and snarly."

Ward was close enough to touch the boy again, but he didn't. "Me, too."

Denny turned to face him. "Well, then, you oughta try and help him."

"I'd like to, Denny. I would. But sometimes things happen and there's nothing you can do—"

"Well, I don't believe that," Denny burst out. "If you really wanted to—you'd try. *I* would. I'd do *something—*" He broke off and added stiffly, "I'd better go on over to the restaurant. Grandma may be worrying about me."

Well, what the hell, Ward thought, watching the boy run off across the parking lot.

The boy's disappointment hurt, more than it should. He was letting them both, Denny and B.J., get under his skin, doing a little head tripping and fantasizing. Well, he had to cut that shit out. This was the real world here.

He could barely handle his own life. He sure as hell couldn't be some surrogate father figure. If Denny expected him to make the world all rosy and sweet and perfect, he had come to the wrong person, and the sooner he learned his mistake, the better.

Behind him, Ward could feel the wolf's eyes, watching, waiting.

I can't help you, he thought. I can't help anybody.

21

Nola was alone again in the dark storm cellar, but the bright flash of sunlight still danced in her eyes. The outline of the man who had opened the door and looked down into the cellar seemed imprinted there, too.

Not her father.

Frank.

Frank had put her down here. She remembered it all. The snakebite, Frank hitting her with the board. He had tried to kill her. Tried . . . why hadn't he finished the job?

Have to get out of here.

Stand up. No, tried that before. A big flop, that performance. Never play in Peoria. She would crawl, then. She could do that. Even babies can crawl.

First she would have to turn over on her stomach. Such a simple thing, but as soon as she moved she heard the river muttering, felt the dark water rising up—easy, easy—the movement hurt, but she had to do it—had to—and then she was turning, falling, the floodwaters roaring in and sweeping her away . . .

Goddamn you, Chuck, why did you go off and leave me here alone?

B.J. snapped awake with a strange, unanchored feeling. She was in her mother's living room, but the room seemed like a small dark cavern, with walls and ceiling pressing in. For an instant she thought she smelled an odor of dank, mushroomy earth, but that was impossible. Not in Iris's immaculate house.

She struggled to sit up, blinking in the spill of yellow sunlight from the window. The simple motion took so much effort it scared her. When she changed the bandage earlier, she had noticed that the cut was healing nicely. Her arm was a little sore, of course, but nothing explained her weakness, or the sleep that was really more like slipping into unconsciousness.

There was one explanation, if she was willing to accept it. Something terrible had happened to Nola: an injury that sent her into deep shock and kept her hovering on the edge of death. And, somehow, B.J. was sharing the experience.

B.J. couldn't deny it anymore. It was true. Admitting that, what if Nola dies? Would their contact snap like an umbilical cord breaking? Or would the connection stay, dragging her down with Nola into the grave?

Wanna find out? she asked herself grimly.

A little psychic experiment. Just lie here on the couch and do nothing.

B.J. forced herself to get up, went out to the kitchen, and made a strong cup of coffee, instant mixed with tap water. Caffeine was the object, not the taste. She'd lost track of time, but according to the kitchen clock, it was only one-thirty. She wasn't hungry, but she knew she ought to have some food. She ate a chicken leg and a slice of bread, forcing herself to chew and swallow.

Then she went upstairs, rubber legged, but never mind. She had already decided what she was going to do back there in the Crossroads' parking lot when she asked

Denny if he wanted to stay behind, so might as well get on with it. She scrubbed her face, brushed her teeth, gathered up car keys, and counted the remaining money in her purse.

Downstairs, she hesitated, then went back to the kitchen and picked up the telephone. At the Crossroads Al answered, asked several concerned questions about her wound, then finally put Iris on.

"Mama, I don't have the strength to argue with you about this, so please just listen," B.J. said. "I'm leaving right now and driving over to Chester."

She heard her mother's swift intake of breath. *"B.J.—"*

"I may find nothing and come right back. In any case, I'll call you tonight. Tell Denny I'm sorry I couldn't wait to talk to him about it, but I had to go. Tell him—" No point asking Iris to explain. A keeper of secrets never does. "Tell him I love him."

She hung up. Almost immediately the phone began to ring. She could still hear it ringing, outside with the front door locked behind her, until she was in the pickup driving away.

Seconds passed. Or hours. Nola had no idea how long.

For the first time she realized that she must be badly hurt and knew she had to take a look at the damage. Daylight leaked in around the door, so the darkness wasn't complete, more of a deep gray gloom.

Nola steeled herself, remembering the jagged board in Frank's hand chopping down at the snake, the moist raw meat of the snake's severed body.

Look, dammit.

No gaping wounds. Her legs were still attached. Tears of relief streamed down her face. A huge bruise blackened her puffy right ankle. She could see that, and she certainly could feel it. Wriggling her toes sent a flash of agony shooting up her leg.

There was an ominous swelling in her lower arm where

the snake's fangs had sunk in. A broken ankle, a little infection—if that was all, no big deal. As for the blow to her head—it didn't pay to think about that or to think about how horribly weak she was.

She had managed to turn over on her stomach before she passed out the last time. Now all she had to do was crawl over and drag herself up the steps—three steps, she remembered that, even after all these years—and push up the door.

All . . . Jesus. And, assuming she could get the door open, where was Frank?

Maybe he was sitting out there, waiting, like a cat beside a mouse hole. Like a crocodile lying, half submerged, in a stream with only his knobs of eyes showing.

She strained to hear some telltale movement. She heard faint rustlings. Not from outside. In the cellar. The gloom had brightened a little, and her eyes were adjusted to the half-light. Still she could not see into the corners of the cellar or under the low benches that bordered the wall.

Her heart accelerated; a painful dry flop echoed up through her head and sent her teetering toward the flood-waters. . . .

Nola willed herself not to fall; the effort was long and excruciating. And when she opened her eyes again, the cavelike cellar had grown perceptibly darker. How long before sunset?

Her monstrous thirst told her she had already spent a night here. She was certain she'd been here a whole day. Aunt Vee would surely be looking for her. And the police—County? State?

In L.A. you had a constant awareness of law enforcement. If you weren't sitting dead-stopped in a massive traffic jam on the freeway, you were driving seventy-five mph and keeping a lookout for the highway patrol in your rearview mirror. At night you regularly heard the drone of the County Sheriff's helicopters and saw the bright sweep of their patrol floodlights.

Chester used to have a policeman when she was a child. Marshall Dillon, the kids called him, an old man with a beer belly who stood as a crossing guard in front of the school and who came when somebody threw a baseball through a neighbor's window. Aside from a lone patrol car on I-55 on the way from the Memphis airport, she hadn't seen a single cop since arriving in Arkansas. But there had to be police. And Aunt Vee would call them, unless Frank talked her out of it somehow.

Nola had seen the kind of influence the man had on her aunt. This was different. Nola had disappeared. They were family, after all. Blood counted.

Then why hadn't Aunt Vee found her? She knew Nola was going back and forth to the old homeplace. The island should have been the first place she looked.

If she looked.

Nola heard another rustling, fainter this time but somehow more ominous. Mice, rats, snakes, things only half imagined. The hundreds of horror movies Chuck dragged her to see filled her mind with monstrous possibilities. Make-believe. Yes. But good horror was rooted in reality. That was a basic tenet of the shock master's trade.

(dark things live in dark places)

And through the thin slit around the door, Nola saw the light changing. She thought it was midafternoon, but how could she be sure? She was only certain of one thing. Night was coming.

(and dark things always come at night to feed)

Crawl. Never mind the pain. Move. Legs. Arms. You're a Douglas, and Douglas women don't give up, come hell or high water.

One inch.

Two.

Hell she could manage, but then the flood came back, and she was no Dorothy Douglas after all, because it picked her right off the high porch and sucked her down, under the black, black waves.

22

Walking back to his car along the river, Frank was glad he let the snake swim away. He had to watch himself, sorting out the things he did for enjoyment from those that fit into his careful plans. From the way Nola looked, another night in the cellar would be enough to finish her off.

Back in Chester, Frank went straight to the Drop Inn for a beer, then back to his room to shower and change before going on over to Verna's. If it were up to him, he wouldn't have taken the time to bathe. The beer had already cooled him off just fine, and odors never bothered him.

He had grown up in squalor in a two-room shack on a hardscrabble farm in eastern Tennessee. Water came from an outside pump. The toilet was an outhouse, drawing hordes of flies in summer. By nature slovenly and lazy, his mother had at least made a halfhearted effort to keep the place clean. But the summer Frank was seven, she announced she was fed up with his father's drinking and whoring and took off for Nashville.

Left mostly to fend for themselves, Frank and his two younger brothers and baby sister quickly became as feral as abandoned cats. Their father vanished for weeks at a time to pick peaches in Georgia or poach alligators in Florida. When he was home, he really didn't care what a shithole the place was as long as they left him alone to sleep off his hangovers.

By the time a horrified social worker packed off the younger children to a foster home and Frank went to live with Uncle Toover, the kids had turned the house into something like a cave inhabited by Cro Magnons. Filth crusted walls and layered floors. Fat white weevils lived in the cupboards and infested flour and cereals. Mice roomed with the weevils, sleek and well-fed from feasting on uncovered garbage.

Over the years Frank had learned to accommodate society with baths, deodorant, and daily changes of clothing. But to tell the truth he still preferred the natural stench of sweat and urine to the smell of soap and perfume. Between projects he liked to rent a fishing shack on Fontana Lake in the Smokies and spend a couple of weeks alone, unshaven and unwashed.

He thought about another one of those little trips, as he pulled into Verna's driveway. This job was taking a lot longer than he had expected. By the time he finished off Verna, he would definitely need a vacation.

She saw his car and was waiting by the door, ready to pounce.

"Where in the world have you been?" she demanded. "I even went by Miss Hopper's looking for you."

"Sorry. I was fishing and the time got away from me. What's wrong?"

"Nola, of course." She went to slump down in the wingback chair. She wore a pink-flowered muumuu that settled tentlike around her. Her sullen mouth wore a sweat mustache.

"Now what did she do?" Frank asked.

"She didn't *do* anything. That's the problem. I called and called. Must've left a dozen messages on that machine of hers. But do you think she called me back?"

127

"Oh, she will, sooner or later," Frank said soothingly.

She took a shoebox off the lamp table beside the chair and held it on her lap.

"Well, I hope so," she said. "Mr. Lasker was on the phone early this morning. He got an offer for the farm property. A really good offer, too."

"So go ahead and sell your half. You don't need to talk to Nola for that."

He eyed the shoebox. He had no idea what was inside, but he knew he wasn't going to like it.

"Well, that's just it," Verna said. "The man wants *all* of the land, the whole thing. If I don't get hold of Nola, I'm going to lose out, Frank. That thoughtless girl—I'm telling you, I won't put up with it. I'll figure out some way to get in touch with her, you'll see."

Oh, crap, Frank thought. He had seen that stubborn, solid look on her face before. She meant to have her way, whatever the cost. One more night, that's all he needed. Just one more night.

"She probably went to work," he said. "It's two hours earlier on the West Coast, don't forget. I'm sure she'll call you when she gets home."

"Why would she go to work if she's planning to move back here?"

"Maybe she changed her mind."

"All those phone calls she made asking about estimates to fix up the place—she sounded pretty set to me. She told me one time she uses a remote beeper and checks her messages every couple of hours. She knows I called, all right. She's just being a stinker about it."

Verna took the lid off the shoebox and began sorting through it. Letters, he saw. A whole box full of them.

"She gave me an emergency number one time when Mama had a bad spell," Verna went on. "Some friend of hers. It's in here someplace. She said this woman had a key to her place. So if this person doesn't know where to reach Nola, well, I'm going to have her go over to Nola's condo, let herself in, and leave a great big sign by the telephone, telling Nola to call me."

"You can't do that," Frank burst out.

She looked up, startled. "Why not? Nola gave me the number. And this is an emergency."

"Well—" He rummaged frantically for a reason. "If she's planning to move back here, she may not even *want* to sell."

"But it's a good price, Frank. Surprisingly good, that's what Mr. Lasker said."

"See, that's my point. If it's that good, maybe she *will* take it. But you two haven't been hitting it off so well, Verna. If you start giving her what for, if you send friends over to bug her, she might say no to the deal just to be nasty."

Verna was not convinced, but at least she stopped thumbing through the box. "She'd be cutting off her nose to spite her face. She's not that stupid." Verna went back to the letters.

"You may be right. You probably are. But what I'm saying is, what can it hurt to wait a couple of hours?"

"I don't *want* to wait," Verna said mulishly. "I don't want to take the chance that this buyer will just up and say to heck with it, I'll buy some other farm. I'm tired of waiting, Frank. I want my money, and I want us to get married, and I want you to take me to Hawaii like you promised."

She pawed frantically through the box. Her face looked like it was swelling up, and she was turning bright red. Jesus. With his luck she would have a stroke and die intestate—just the thought of that word made him shudder.

"Verna, honey, now I want you to calm down—"

"It's not here!" she cried. "I know I put it away—I *remember*—"

"Verna," he said sternly, "you listen to me. You're all upset over nothing." He took the box from her. "I want you to sit there and relax. Take some deep breaths. I'm going to go make you something cold to drink. Some cherry Kool-Aid, your favorite. Then we'll talk about this and figure out what to do, okay?"

She nodded.

"Okay, then."

In the kitchen he mixed Kool-Aid, adding extra sugar the way Verna liked it, and wished he dared risk ducking upstairs and raiding the store of drugs in old Dorothy's medicine cabinet. Sheer luck had granted him a short reprieve, but he knew Verna wouldn't give up so easily.

She reminded him of a python. If one locked its jaws around your arm, well, either you'd better figure on cutting off your arm or dismembering the damn thing because it would never let go.

He poured the Kool-Aid over ice. Get her started on this one, then he would go up for some Valium, that ought to slow her down. He took the glass and went into the living room.

Verna wasn't there.

Just as he had known the shoebox meant trouble, he knew that empty wingback chair spelled disaster even before he saw the door next to the stairs standing ajar—the door to the basement. He walked over and stood in front of the open door, the icy glass sweating and cold moisture running down his wrist, an even colder premonition slithering down his spine.

He waited, sipping the Kool-Aid, a dozen contingency plans leaping, fully detailed, into his mind, the most likely one that he would shove Verna backward down the basement steps, make sure her neck was broken, then be long gone before the cops arrived.

He heard a thump of heavy footsteps, then Verna appeared, her pink-flowered muumuu smudged with dirt, a gray cobweb caught in her hair.

"Another box," she gasped. "I remembered and I went down to look and—Frank, somebody put Nola's suitcases in the basement. Somebody—" She broke off. Her face was no longer crimson. It was sickly pale. *"Frank?"*

Still deciding, he put a hand on her arm. No need to rush into things. He gave her a tug toward him.

"Come on, Verna," he said. "We have to talk."

For a long time Frank sold gold-embossed Bibles and aluminum siding, until he realized how easy it was to sell himself to the lonely, unattractive women who made up the bulk of his clientele. Over the past twenty-five years he had persuaded thirty-two women to turn over jewelry, bearer bonds, savings accounts, and, once, a cache of Maple Leafs and Krugerrands to his keeping, marrying the women if necessary to close the deal. Uncle Toover's revival meetings had taught him a lot more than how to handle snakes.

The trick of the selling job, he discovered, was to tell the woman what she wanted to hear. So now he told Verna that he loved her and reminded her of the wonderful life they had planned once her mother was gone, how she deserved that life, and how, if he had anything to say about it, she was, by God, going to get that life.

"If I've made a mistake, if I've done something some people might think was wrong, it's because of our love and my dreams of our future together," he said earnestly. "I only hope and pray you'll remember that."

She jerked her head in a nod, puppetlike, her gaze riveted to his face. He had led her back to the sofa and sat beside her, holding her hands in both of his, looking directly into her eyes.

"I knew Nola would be out at the old house yesterday," he went on. "I drove out there to talk to her. I had some idea of reminding her how you took care of your mother all these years, doing all the dirty work. Well, she'd said so herself, but I thought if I put it to her straight, maybe shame her a little, she'd see how unfair that will was. Oh, I know it was a dumb idea, but, sweetheart, seeing you so upset and knowing what it meant to both of us, well, I had to *try*.

"It was a lost cause, of course. I knew it right away. She was even nastier than she was to you. We were outside walking around. She got it in her head that she wanted to see what was inside that old storm cellar. Said she couldn't get the door open and would I do it for her. So I did."

Now came the clincher. If he expected Verna to buy it, he'd better make it good.

"And that's when it happened, when I was lifting the door. She started screaming she'd been snake-bit, crying Jesus, Jesus, and stumbling around. By then I had the door up and it happened so fast, Verna—not a damn thing I could do—well, she fell headfirst down into the cellar. She hurt herself pretty bad."

Verna surprised him, cutting straight through to the heart of the matter. "Is she dead?"

"Not yet."

Her eyes were like two peepholes. Frank looked inside and saw the machinery turning in her head. Yeah, Verna, figure it out. If Nola dies, the clause in Dorothy's will takes effect, so you'll get everything. All that money, the trip to Hawaii, a cruise to Jamaica, a townhouse in Memphis—what else had he dangled in front of her?

"Do you think she's really going to die?" Verna asked faintly.

"Oh, yeah," Frank said. "I certainly do."

23

During the long California summers and the endless bright falls, especially when the Santa Ana winds came helling in off the desert, there were times when Nola began to hate sunlight so intensely that she would spend her Sundays closeted in the condo with the blinds tightly drawn, studying the weather page in the *Los Angeles Times,* looking for the cloudiest, wettest places in the world, and planning to go there. Twice, in the past five years, when she had the time and the money, she flew up to Vancouver and was rewarded with rain.

Now, in the storm cellar with that thin fine line of illumination slowly fading, she knew with primal certainty what the sun really meant—safety, a fiery barrier against the horrors of the night.

There had been more ominous rustlings underneath the benches. Once she thought she saw movement and a gleam of shiny, slitted eyes. Terror kept her moving and she had made it to the steps, an inch at a time.

She lost count of how many times the floodwaters rushed in. Once Annie came to comfort her, and once Grandma sat on the top step, coaxing her on.

"You think it was easy, staying out here all alone?"

Dorothy Douglas had said. "The water rising and more rain coming down. But I wouldn't give up, no sir, and if you've got any backbone, you won't, either."

Drifting away on the floodwaters was not giving up, Nola told herself. The first step loomed above her; it seemed a story high. She decided to rest a few minutes before she tackled it.

Lying there, she heard the rumble in the ground before she actually identified the sound of the car's engine. *Frank.* Oh, God, he was coming back. A louder rumble, then the engine stopped. Car doors slammed.

I have to keep still, very still, and maybe—

Maybe what? He'd forget she was here?

And what if it wasn't Frank? It might be Aunt Vee, or the police—of course! Twenty-four hours, that was always the time period on the cop shows. Some desk sergeant saying sternly, "She's not a missing person for twenty-four hours, ma'am, that's the law."

"Here. I'm in here. Aunt Vee—" She called over and over, but, oh, God, such a faint croak they would never hear her through the thick earthen walls.

She needed noise, something to attract their attention. A stick, to hammer on the wooden steps. There was nothing within reach, so she drummed with her fist—a real boomer—Jesus, like an ant jumping up and down on a piano key.

Above her the storm cellar door creaked open.

Light flared. Not so bad this time, the sun not so bright, and instantly blocked by a bulky silhouette. Still, it took a long maddening moment to make out who stood there.

"Aunt Vee?"

Tears wet her cheeks. Her whole body went limp with relief as she waited for Aunt Vee to come down and to tell her everything would be all right.

But Verna just stood there, saying nothing. Her silence clamped a chill hand on Nola's heart.

"Aunt Vee?" she whispered. "Please . . ."

Nola's pupils had dropped down now, accommodating the change in light, and she saw a man stepping up behind Verna, peering over her shoulder. Frank.

Verna turned to him and said, "All right. I've seen enough."

She stepped back, and Frank closed the door.

Nola screamed then, *"No, no, NOOOO,"* the sound ripping her throat, and she hitched her way up one step, grabbing the edge of the rough wood and heaving her body up.

I'll show you. I'll get to the goddamn door by myself.

All she opened were the floodgates, sending the black water crashing in. In the midst of the tidal swirl and the mutter of the wave, she heard another sound and knew exactly what it was: an engine starting, Aunt Vee and Frank driving away.

B.J. pulled off to the side of the road outside Chester and gripped the steering wheel while the world went all wonky, as Iris used to say when B.J. was little. Yeah, all wonky and sideways and upside-down. Sweet Jesus.

Just knowing that the blackouts had a psychic rather than a physical source had helped her to fight them off. During the drive over, across the Mississippi and down through the Missouri bootheel, she had willed strength back into her arms and legs, and she had felt fine. Well, not really *fine,* but at least not like a bowl of soft-set Jello.

Now this. Black despair. Energy draining away at an alarming rate. *Nola . . .*

Forget it. Let go or you'll drown with her.

Yes, that was exactly what the sensation felt like, being clutched by a drowning person while they were both sucked down into a whirlpool of black water. So, do what you have to do. Push her away. Break her hold.

Swim, she told herself.

And Denny, think about Denny. His sweet open face. His total unquestioning joy in life. Denny without a mother if she didn't get her shit together.

A car drove past, slowed, and the driver gave her a curious look.

"I'm okay," she said—to herself. The other car was already gone.

She eased the truck into gear and pulled out onto the road. She was shaky, and she could feel that terrible lethargy pooling, dark as swamp water, as she drove into town.

Keeping her son's face firmly fixed in her mind, B.J. found Chester's one lone Conoco station and stopped to ask directions to Verna Douglas's house.

24

Verna had been stone silent all the way home, hunched over, double chin sunk into her neck, staring straight ahead through the windshield. At home she transferred the pose to the wingback chair, sitting mute and scared while Frank went upstairs for a handful of Valium—just in case.

She still sat that way when he came downstairs. He told her he was going to get them something cold to drink and went out to the kitchen for the Kool-Aid, stirring one 10-milligram tablet into her glass. No sense taking chances.

He knew it was a mistake taking her to the old house, but she had insisted with her usual mulish stubbornness.

"I need to see for myself," she had said. "If you won't take me, I'll go anyway."

In the living room she took the glass without question, her hand trembling, and sipped.

He waited patiently, keeping his options open.

"She looks pretty bad," Verna said finally.

"Yes, she does."

"I don't know. . . . I don't think I can just—just leave

137

her there." She slopped a few drops of Kool-Aid on her muumuu, the red liquid blending right in with the pink print.

"I know it's hard," Frank said. "But I really don't think she's suffering much. I think she's unconscious most of the time."

Now for the closer; he gave it his best shot. "Sweetheart, listen to me. You have a warm, generous heart, but you let people take advantage of your loving nature. My God, when I think of all those years you sacrificed taking care of your mother—" He shook his head, letting the wonder of it show. "You were the one who was on twenty-four-hour call. Not Nola. Where was Nola when Dorothy messed in her bed, or when she spent nights at a time yelling for you because she was afraid to go to sleep?

"Then what do you get for all your love and care? Nola marches in here and takes half of what should be rightfully yours. Now fate has stepped in. Fate will change that mistake, if you'll let it. For once in your life, sweetheart, you have to think of yourself."

"But what if somebody finds her?" Verna asked. "She'll tell them how we came out there and didn't help her."

"There is always that chance," he admitted. "I don't think it's very likely, but say it happens. We did go out there. Of course we didn't see Nola. We were looking around because of the offer on the property. As far as we knew she was in Los Angeles. She must have heard us talking, and she just imagined we opened that door. She was hallucinating, poor thing."

"I guess so." Verna held the Kool-Aid steady now. He could see her brain clicking away. "But what about her clothes? She doesn't have them with her and if they search here . . ."

Sharp, he thought, a little chagrined to find a hole in his careful plans.

"We'll take the suitcases out there tonight and put

them in her car. It will look like she was on her way to the airport and wanted one last look at the old house. If we ever have to explain, well, she had a nasty bump on the head. No wonder she doesn't remember planning to leave. What you have to keep in mind, sweetheart, is that it's her word against both of ours."

"If she lives," Verna said.

"If she does."

"What if she doesn't? How will we explain it to the police that I wasn't puzzled when she didn't call from L.A.? Or why I wasn't worried when I couldn't reach her?"

"Well, you *were* worried. Then we finally figured out she didn't make it to L.A., so naturally we went looking for her. And when we found her—a terrible accident, that's what we tell them. That's what it was, Verna."

"It could work." She'd finished the drink. Her face had a loose, slack look, her pupils slightly dilated. "We could get married and sell this place, too, and move to Memphis and—"

The doorbell rang. Verna broke off, instantly confused, her eyes lit by a dim terror as she struggled to get up, gasping, "Oh, no, oh, God, the police—we're not ready."

"Just stay there," Frank said. "I'll take care of it."

B.J. knew how these little towns were laid out, with meandering streets and, just to make things interesting, missing street signs and very few houses which displayed numbers, so she asked for specific directions at the gas station. Even at that, she drove past the Douglas house and had to turn around.

The house was two stories high, made of rosy red brick, sitting in the middle of a tree-shrouded lot with a kind of staid dignity.

A late model Buick sat in the driveway along with an old Pontiac and a pickup truck with a camper shell similar to her own. A decal on the pickup's door read *Mr.*

Fix-It. A man dressed in jeans and a gray T-shirt—Mr. Fix-It, she guessed—stood on the front stoop talking to somebody inside the house. A man, she saw, but she didn't get a good look before the door closed. Mr. Fix-It walked back to his truck, looking disappointed.

B.J. parked on the street and went up the asphalt driveway. A man opened the door before she could ring the bell. Probably the same person who just sent Mr. Fix-It on his way. He was short, simian dark, with flat muddy eyes.

"If you're here about the remodeling job, I'm afraid you've wasted your time," he said.

Her skin creeped as his gaze lingered on the low curve of her tank top.

"I dropped by to see Nola. Is she home?"

"Nola?" His eyes shuttered closed, but not before B.J. saw the startled flicker. "Sorry, she's not here."

"Oh, that's too bad. I was in town visiting my cousin. Nola and I went to school together." B.J. hadn't planned on the glib lies. They just tumbled out. "I heard Nola came for her grandmother's funeral."

"Yes, that's right. But I'm afraid she left. Went back to L.A."

"Oh, shoot. That's a shame. Is her aunt Verna here?"

"No, she—"

"Frank, who is it? I thought you sent that man away."

A plump woman wearing an awful muumuu walked into the small entry, moving with a peculiar gait as though she was having trouble keeping her balance.

She stared at B.J. "Who is it? What do you want? Frank?"

"Go on back and sit down," Frank said. "I'll handle it."

Drunk, B.J. thought. Taking a chance, she said, "Miss Douglas? Remember me? It's B.J.—" Johnson might ring a bell, so she quickly added, "B.J. Jones. I just wanted to say hi to Nola."

"Nola's not here. Tell her, Frank. Tell her Nola's gone."

Something about the eyes—not drunk. Stoned, B.J. thought. Stoned and scared witless.

"Verna's had a rough time since her mother died," Frank said. "She can't talk to you right now."

"Maybe I'll stop by tomorrow—"

"That's not a good idea. We'll tell Nola you were here." He shut the door.

I blew it, B.J. thought as she trudged down the driveway.

She should have asked them about Nola's mom and dad. Did they live around here too? At least she could have told them who she was, why she had come, her fears about Nola. Oh, sure, and maybe Aunt Verna would have shared her tranks while they all waited for the men in the white suits.

Anyway there was something about those two she didn't trust.

In the truck she sat for a minute, trying to decide what to do next. Go on back to Tennessee, that was the logical thing. She didn't know a soul in Chester. All she had was a bunch of Mama's old memories to guide her. She could wander around and ask questions, but she knew these small towns. When people started poking noses into anybody's business, they clammed up fast.

Driving away, she glanced down at the gas gauge. She needed fuel soon. The prices were so high here, but did she have enough gas to get back to Blytheville? Better not chance it. On the main street, approaching the Conoco station, she decided she would just buy a couple of gallons.

Mr. Fix-It was there, too, filling his tank.

He was lean and tanned. The gray T-shirt had the sleeves cut off to reveal ropy muscles and the tattoo of an eagle on his upper arm. He lit up a cigarette, ignoring the NO SMOKING sign, and leaned against the fender while the gasoline pump clicked off tenths of gallons. As she climbed down from her pickup, he gave her the once-over, his glance lingering.

One last shot, B.J. thought, and said casually, "Hi. I saw you over at the Douglases. You were leaving as I was arriving."

"Yeah?" He squinted through curling smoke.

Terrific, probably the only good ole boy in the South who didn't like to gab. "I dropped by to say hello to Nola, but she'd left for L.A."

"So they said. You have any idea when she's coming back?"

"No, I'm afraid not."

"Damn," he said glumly. "I knew it was too good to be true."

"What's that, Bob?" The lone attendant came around the back of B.J.'s truck, wiping his hands on a greasy rag. Not the same man B.J. had asked for directions. He looked at Bob's—Mr. Fix-It's—cigarette and shook his head. "Jesus, Bob."

Bob dropped the cigarette and ground it out with his heel. "Old Miz Douglas's granddaughter—she had some nutty idea about living out there on Painter's Island, doing the whole place over."

"Yeah?" The attendant shook his head in disbelief. "I hear she's got a fancy job out in Hollywood. Why in the world would she wanna move back here?"

"Guess she don't," Bob said. "Put the gas on my bill, will you?"

He got in the truck, lifted a hand in a good-bye salute, and drove off.

"Fill 'er up, ma'am?" the attendant said.

A two-gallon sale might not prompt much information. "Five dollars' worth." Not much better, but all she could afford. Her thoughts raced, but she tried to sound cool as she mentioned stopping by to see Nola.

"That right?" he said. "Nola Douglas a friend of yours?"

"Yes, I was sorry to miss her. Did you see her at all when she was here?"

"Not to talk to. Just at the funeral. Old Miz Douglas had a real nice send-off."

"So I heard. Were Nola's parents there?"

"No. Her daddy's dead, of course." He gave B.J. a dubious look.

"I meant her mom and stepfather," B.J. said hastily.

"Didn't come. Stayed out in California, I guess." He finished pumping and held out his hand for the money.

Now what? Maybe the island. That was the only place she and Nola had ever been together all those years ago. Going there would probably be a waste of time. Still—"Nola told me about Painter's Island, and I'm curious. Can you tell me how to find it?"

He could—sort of. She got the general idea, paid him from her dwindling reserve, and blew seventy-five cents on a can of Dr Pepper to take along and drink in the truck.

Behind her in the west the sun hung just above the trees. A good two hours of daylight left. Plenty of time to find the place and look around. Not that she expected to turn up anything. If Nola left to go back to L.A., she would have flown out of Memphis. And if she was in trouble she could be anywhere along the route between Chester and the airport. Or in L.A. in her own apartment lying in a pool of blood, unable to answer the phone.

But I have to start looking somewhere, B.J. thought as she drove over the first levee and headed toward the Mississippi.

After two false turns that resulted in deadends, she backtracked to the ramshackled liquor store. Both the proprietor and his skinny gray dog eyed her with the country suspicion of strangers, but the man grudgingly gave her directions.

This time B.J. found the island. As she drove over the pontoon bridge, the sun hovered on the horizon, a distorted orange globe. She saw a building through the trees. The road curved, and there was the old house as ugly as her mother had described it, squatting in the shadows, windows glowing dully with the sunset light like ancient eyes.

Blood ticked in her ears as she parked the car. Atop its high foundation, the house loomed over her. There was no breeze at all. She could smell the river and the green odor of sunbaked weeds.

She walked up the steps and raised her hand to knock, hesitated—the place was so obviously deserted. Probably all locked up—but when she grasped the doorknob, it turned. She went inside.

Stepping into the small living room, her skin prickled and a rush of information flooded her brain. The house had been aired—no, there were still windows open. She could feel a draft. There were footprints in the dust, curtains torn down and left in a heap. And everywhere the sense, the feel, the shape . . . Nola.

Quickly she searched all the rooms, upstairs and down. Closets, a pantry. She found nothing and ended back in the kitchen, where she stood, staring at an old maple rocker, remembering her mother's words.

"I came back in the kitchen, and there was Nola sitting in that rocking chair with you on her lap. . . . "

Was this the same chair? B.J. touched the spindled back and sank down in it. She couldn't possibly remember, yet she did. Not the incident itself, just some elemental sensation of a love so strong it still lingered, resonated, in her memory.

"Nola," she whispered. "It's Annie. Please answer me."

Nothing. Nothing. Still nothing.

And then a ghostly whisper, faint but clear.

"Annie?"

B.J. gripped the chair arms, her heart hammering. "Nola? Nola, where are you? Tell me where to find you. Nola?"

No answer, but B.J. was sure now. Nola wasn't lost somewhere on the road to Memphis or lying injured in L.A. She was right here on the island.

25

She has to learn to swim, goddammit, before she falls in the fucking river and drowns.

Daddy carrying her, striding swiftly toward the river, Mommy running behind, screaming, she's a baby. She's three years old for God's sake.

Nola's screaming too, Daddy, Daddy, I don't wanna, and then they're at the end of the boat dock and Daddy's saying, let go, Nola. You'll be all right. Daddy won't let anything happen to you.

And then he throws her in the river. . . .

The dark water rushed over her just like that day on the boat dock. Daddy had kept his promise then, jumping in and holding out his arms to grab her as she fought and sputtered, flailing wildly and somehow staying afloat. But Daddy wasn't here to catch her now. Nobody was.

She was so tired, so horribly tired. She wanted to stop for a while, to drift and listen to the river's slow, lazy murmur.

But Grandma kept yelling at her, "Get moving, girl. You're a Douglas. Douglas women don't give up."

And Annie was calling for her to come out and play.

No, they *were* playing. Hide and seek. Come out, come out, wherever you are.

I'm here, over here, and I don't wanna play anymore. . . .

B.J. stood on the high front porch and scanned the overgrown yard with its dense second-growth trees crowding in. Nola was here. No more questioning *how* she knew, she just *did.*

Nola must have driven her car to the island, but where was it? Through the trees, orange light gleamed off the water of the slough. B.J. descended the steps and hurried down the road toward the water. Around the curve she could see the bridge.

The construction of the bridge was simple. Two pontoons that looked like the ones on a floatplane formed the basis for the crosspieces topped with two long planks that served as runners for a vehicle's wheels. There were no side rails and no protective barriers.

B.J. broke into a run. Out on the bridge she stopped, breathing hard, and looked down. The water was a dark, sludgy brown, but she could make out vague shapes of roots and discarded cans on the bottom. The slough was too shallow to hide a car.

Frustrated, she stood for a moment, staring back at the trees that sheltered the house, the bridge quivering beneath her feet. Maybe the car was parked around back. Returning to the yard, she noticed that her truck had left tire impressions in earth still soft from the rain.

She studied the ground. More tracks. From the different tire patterns, she could see that at least two cars had been here. There were footprints, too.

B.J. quartered the yard. No sign of the car, but she immediately saw tire tracks leading off into the trees. As she went past the side of the house, she also noticed an earthen mound out in back and recognized it as a storm cellar.

She followed the tracks, ducking low-hanging

branches, and there it was: a red Chevy Beretta with Tennessee plates and a Budget Rent-A-Car sticker on the back bumper.

The door was unlocked. Nobody inside. *Oh, Nola, where are you?* Premonition iced her blood. The car had not driven itself into the trees; it had been hidden here.

She had pictured all kinds of possibilities, many of them bloody but all random with Nola the victim of an accident or a mugging. Now she thought of premeditated evil, the idea instantly creditable and yielding up another likelihood of Nola's whereabouts.

She circled around the Beretta and banged on the trunk with her fist.

"Nola? Nola?"

No response.

She leaned down and laid her ear against the metal. Nothing. But if Nola was weak, she might be unable to respond. B.J. headed back to her pickup to get a tire iron to pry open the trunk, all the while calling to Nola. The reply was faint—so faint—and flickering like a candle flame.

Almost to the pickup, she spotted the storm cellar again. Suddenly she remembered awakening from her nap and feeling that she was in someplace dark and cavelike, smelling dank and moldy.

She veered around the Toyota and broke into a run, stumbling over the lumpy ground, the tall grass whipping against her legs, praying, God, oh, God, let her be there.

Annie, please I don't wanna play anymore.

I'm hanging on to the boat dock, but I'm tired and scared, so scared. Pretty soon I have to let go, and then I'll float away. . . .

Nola heard the door creak open. Vaguely she knew that somebody was there, calling her name.

Then there were arms lifting her, a strange woman holding her and crying, the woman's tears warm and salty on Nola's face.

"It's Annie," the woman said. "I'm here, Nola."

She must be hallucinating again because Annie was a ghost child, not this very real woman who was saying, "I'm going to get you out of here," and half-carried, half-dragged her out into the fading evening light.

"An-nie?"

"Shh, don't try to talk." B.J.'s voice was thick with tears, her cheeks wet, her eyes streaming. Unwilling to let go of Nola, she reached for the tail of her tank top and pressed it against her face.

Nola was lighter by maybe fifteen pounds, but carrying her had been like tugging a sack of cement up those steps. B.J.'s shoulders burned with the effort, and she thought she might have broken open the stitches in her arm. She could see a bright red bloom on the bandage.

None of this mattered a damn compared to Nola's condition. Her head lolled infantlike on B.J.'s breast. B.J. knew where to look, and a quick check revealed the swelling at the base of her skull.

Remembering the pain in her own head, B.J. understood how bad the blow had been. Dried blood trailed from one ear and from the corner of Nola's mouth. One lower leg had ballooned, sausage tight. Nola's arm was also swollen, inflamed with a bad infection.

The injuries were serious,

(mortal)

but it was Nola's corpse-gray coloring made B.J.'s heart clench with despair. That and the terrible lethargy that B.J. knew so well.

"Son of a bitch," B.J. said. "Who did this to you?"

Nola was not in that cellar as a result of an accident, not with the Chevy hidden in the trees and the cellar door barred shut. What else had Nola's attacker done to her? There was no blood on her shorts, but that didn't rule out rape.

Nola whispered something—not a name—"Water,"

she said. My God, of course, her lips were puffy and cracked. She had been in that cellar for more than a day.

"Nola, I'm going to have to leave you here for a minute so I can get the truck. And I'll get you some water. Okay?"

The eyelids fluttered. "Don't—leave—me—"

"Of course I won't leave you," B.J. said fiercely. "I just can't carry you that far, so I'll bring the truck to you. Hang on, you hear me?"

"Douglas." The word was weak but firm. B.J. instinctively finished her sentence: *I'm a Douglas and I damn well never give up.*

Twilight grayed the clearing, colors muted even more by a river mist. Frogs and cicadas sang a deafening chorus. Mosquitoes buzzed around her head. The humid air smelled of mud, green growth, insect resin, and the faint odor of diesel smoke. Far away a barge boat hooted as B.J. reached the pickup and climbed in.

She drove quickly through the overgrown, hummocky yard and parked near the storm cellar, leaving the engine running and the headlights on. She grabbed a water jug from the camper and went back to Nola, who lay in the pool of light.

"Easy does it," B.J. said, tipping the cup and dribbling water into Nola's mouth.

Was there a hospital in Blytheville? At least there would be a doctor. Of course she might be making a terrible mistake moving Nola at all, but she couldn't leave her here alone—unless she had to. Maybe she wouldn't be able to get Nola into the truck. No, screw that. She would. If she got Nola out of the storm cellar, she could damn well finish the job.

A few more drops of water. Magic stuff, because Nola's eyes had lost that glazed look. She stared up at B.J. with wonder.

"Annie?"

"You betcha," B.J. said. "It's me all right. Weird, huh? You ready to get out of here?"

A blink.

"Okay, then. If you can hold on to me at all, it would sure help—"

B.J. broke off. Froze. She knew somebody was there even though she had no idea how she knew it, until she realized that beyond the rumble of the Toyota's engine, the night was suddenly, eerily still.

Nola knew it, too. Her body tensed in B.J.'s arms.

B.J. saw him, then, sidling around the truck's front fender. She knew who it was even before he stepped into the light.

The man who had been with Verna. *Frank,* with a gun in his hand.

"Well," he said, "I see you got to have your reunion with Nola after all."

$=== 26 ===$

True to his word, Denny brought part of his supper to Lobo—a handful of french fries wrapped up in a paper napkin. Ward took the food and put it in the cage, hating the coolness that had sprung up between him and the boy but feeling helpless to do anything about it.

He was relieved when a family with five hyper kids invaded the enclosure. While he made sure that Ebbie avoided major injury, he could see Denny, unnaturally subdued, watching the wolf.

Lobo didn't touch the food. He had moved only once in the past few hours, driven by thirst to go and lap a little water. Now he was back to crouching in a corner of the cage, staring at Ward.

When the customers finally left, Denny regarded the wolf sadly. "Maybe he doesn't like french fries."

"No, maybe not." Ward patted a jittery Ebbie, choosing his words. He had noticed that B.J.'s truck had not reappeared. Noticed, hell. He had been watching for her. "I thought your mom was coming back for you."

"She said she was." Worry creased Denny's forehead. "I think she must be feeling worse."

"Why do you think that?"

"I just do. Grandma said Mom called, and she wasn't coming for me. I asked Grandma what was wrong, but all she'd say was she'd tell me later and not to worry. I *hate* that," Denny said vehemently. "I do worry. I worry all the time, and I can't stop just because she tells me to."

"She's right though. Your mom's probably resting, that's all."

He didn't believe it any more than Denny did. He remembered B.J.'s eyes, looking beyond him into some terrible middle distance.

"I guess so. I gotta go," Denny said. "I think I'll call Mom and see how she's feeling."

Denny looked very young trudging across the parking lot. Watching him, Ward knew that the Ward Trager he used to be—that cocky, self-assured skateboard champion, jock, soldier—would have said, "Fuck this bullshit," and charged off to find out just what was wrong and fix it for the boy. But that arrogant fellow had vanished one day on a jungle trail in a Vietcong ambush that wiped out an entire platoon except for him and Remy and two FNG's who died within the week. This Ward Trager had learned the limits of his power in the most painful way possible.

Sorry, kid, but it's a full-time job keeping your head down and your mouth shut and hanging on to your sanity any way you can.

Business at the zoo tapered off around seven-thirty. Ward was thinking about nipping over to ask Jerry to give him a burger in a take-out bag when he saw Denny bolt from the restaurant. The big fluorescents had come on, casting their sickly blue glow. Denny was headed for the zoo, but he changed direction and ran off around the building.

"Denny?" Ward called.

The boy didn't stop. Ward really didn't think about

what he was doing. He just headed out the enclosure gate and strode across the asphalt, through a swarm of light-frenzied gnats, saying, "Fuck this bullshit."

Denny stood around the corner, back against the building, clutching his middle. Ward saw his shoulders heave. He wanted to gather the boy up in his arms, but he knew that nine-year-olds don't react well to being treated like a baby.

So he didn't touch Denny. Instead, he dropped down on his heels, which put him on Denny's level. "I'd like to know what's wrong when you want to tell me."

Then he waited. Denny sobbed. Not much, just a few constricted, gasping sounds.

He finally said, "Mom—l-l-left."

"What do you mean?"

"She went off and left me," Denny said bitterly. "Just like my dad."

Ward was prepared to hear that B.J. was in the hospital, or in a psycho ward, but he didn't believe that she had deserted her son. "Oh, Denny, no. You must have misunderstood. What happened exactly?"

"I wanted to call, to see how she was. I told you, I was worried. But when I asked Grandma for money for the phone, she said never mind, that Mom wasn't there. That she went over to Arkansas. To visit some friends, she said."

"Well, then—what's wrong with that? Maybe she needed a day or two to herself."

"It's a buncha crap," Denny cried. "Me and Mom— we're a team. We go everywhere *together*. And we don't have friends in Arkansas. We got customers, that's all. She musta left me, Mr. Trager, or else she's got something really wrong with her or—"

"Denny!" It was Jerry sticking his head around the corner. "Your grandma says to get back in here. She don't want you out there in the dark."

The boy went, head down, and Ward let him go. It wasn't his business for Chrissake, and even if he offered to help, he could imagine Iris Johnson's reaction. She wouldn't want any help from the likes of him, thank you very much.

He wished he could talk to Iris, to find out what had really happened. He still couldn't imagine that B.J. would abandon her son, although, of course, he should be able to believe it. God knows these past years he'd seen his share of sick, mean people and their endless atrocities, so nothing should surprise him.

He walked slowly back to the enclosure, and emotions he had kept bottled up for years rose like blisters. He turned off the lights and put up the CLOSED sign. If Raylene didn't like it, well, fuck it, he didn't give a good goddamn.

He let Ebbie and the Merinos into the pasture and opened the door to the wolf's run, but the wolf only crouched, eyes mirroring mad slivers of blue-violet light. Then Ward went to get his supper. Two burgers, he told Jerry. Fries. And some of that day-old, lard-laden apple pie. Put it on my tab.

Out of sight, waiting for his grease ration, he heard voices, Raylene, near the swinging doors, saying, "I really don't care if that daughter of yours runs off and dumps her kid on you, but I do care when it affects this restaurant."

"What my daughter does is no concern of yours," Iris said. "Now I'm taking my grandson home so he can go to bed. If you don't want me back tomorrow, why, all you have to do is say so."

"What's going on?" Al, coming into the conversation.

"I expect your wife will tell you," Iris said stiffly. "You can call me and let me know what you decide."

Jerry rolled his eyes at Ward as he handed him his take-out bag. "'Ja hear that? Didn't know ole Iris had it in her."

Ward took his burgers and his sleeping bag and his bottle of cheap bourbon down to the far end of the pasture. He saw Iris's Dodge leave the parking lot, and he lifted the bottle and drank a toast to an old broad who had more guts than he'd given her credit for.

The whiskey lit a harsh fire in his stomach. He ate only part of a burger. Why spoil a good drunk? He thought about giving the rest of his supper to the wolf, but he knew the animal wouldn't eat it.

Ward rarely drank, so the liquor went to his head quickly. He'd avoided alcoholism—God knows why, but he had—keeping the bottle for the worst nights, nights like this one.

Before dawn ghosts would be on the prowl. All those Ward Tragers who were or might have been. Mom and Dad with their disappointment that had turned to an abiding sadness. FNG's with legs blown off by claymores. Platoon leaders who had just begun to shave, their baby faces quickly turned old. The Cong—oh, shit, yes—lots of Cong.

And Remy. Always Remy.

Ward would need the bottle tonight.

=27=

Keeping the gun trained on the two women, Frank reached inside the pickup's open window and switched off the ignition key. He left the lights on. No sense stumbling around in the dark. He had driven his Pontiac down the dirt road toward the island with his lights off, parked it a good quarter mile away, and walked in. Good thing, too. And good thing he had started feeling uneasy after B.J. left Verna's and had decided to come out here to check on things.

Nola was still alive, cradled in B.J.'s arms. Her eyes stared at him, a doe's eyes, trapped. She croaked something to B.J. Something like "It's him."

"I know, it's all right," B.J. said, then to Frank, "Please. She's in bad shape. We have to get her to a doctor."

"You're asking me to *help* her? That's pretty silly, wouldn't you say?"

"I'm asking you to think about what you're doing. It's not too late. You can turn around and walk away."

"Right. And I suppose you would never tell anybody I was here."

"I won't. I promise—*please*—"

"Just shut the fuck up."

A pleasant rage rose inside him. He could shoot the bitch in the kneecaps. It might be worth the risk of somebody hearing the gunshots. Better still, he could choke the life out of her—slowly. Of course, doing that might screw up his plans. He couldn't keep things straight with the image of his hands around her neck taking over his thoughts.

"You're not going to get away with this," B.J. said. "I figured it out. I came here. Somebody else will, too. People know where I am."

She had balls, Frank had to give her that, but she was afraid, too. Oh, yes, he could smell the fear, so he was sure she was lying and nobody knew she was here.

He considered. What he needed right now was time to think. To plan. And he had Verna to reckon with. She was back at the house, snoring on the couch, but she wouldn't sleep forever.

Behind the women the storm cellar door gaped open like a dark mouth. He motioned with the gun. "Okay, get up and start dragging your friend back to the cellar."

"No," Nola moaned.

"Listen, please," B.J. said. "I told you, she needs a doctor. She—"

"No, *you* listen. She's going back in the cellar. Now, are you going with her, or am I going to put a bullet in your head and dump you in the river?"

She got up and lifted Nola, grimacing in pain. She had a bandage on her arm, and old Nola was a dead weight— just not quite dead enough, he thought with a wolfish grin.

He settled back against the bumper of the pickup to watch the fun.

B.J. backed down the cellar steps as carefully as she could. The muscles in her shoulders burned, and her arm throbbed, but the pain was nothing compared to the terror of being trapped down here. Her brain raced trying to think of some way to stop it from happening.

Throw dirt in Frank's eyes, rush him and take her chances—the problem was B.J. knew the sawed-off little monster would not only do what he had promised, he would enjoy shooting her.

"Annie?" Nola's face was chalky, her breathing shallow.

"It's all right. We'll be okay." B.J. tried to believe it, but then she got a glimpse of Frank's vicious face just before the cellar door thumped closed and the bar clunked into place.

Nola clutched her and keened. "Flood. High— waters—"

"No, no. At least we don't have to worry about that. It's not even raining. Shhh, rest now."

B.J. held Nola, rocking her a little. The cellar was dark except for a narrow light around the door from the Toyota's headlights. And if Frank turned them off . . .

He did, and then the cellar was pitch black. She strained to listen. Had he gone away? She thought he probably had. She waited, taking deep breaths and trying to calm her thoughts. When she was sure a good five minutes had passed, that he must have left, she whispered reassurances to Nola, eased her down, and went up to push against the door, hoping to dislodge the bar. It was securely fastened.

B.J. felt a wave of despair. Earlier she'd gotten a look at the inside of the cellar, and now as she felt the rough wood around the door, her fingers confirmed what she'd seen. The ceiling was made of old, splintery planking that formed an igloolike structure.

Her probing only loosened the dirt in a crack and sent it showering into her hair. There might be a loose board somewhere, but without a glimmer of light, all she was going to get was a handful of slivers.

Below her Nola cried out. "Annie!"

159

"Here." B.J. went quickly and gathered Nola into her arms.

"Dream," Nola whispered. "I thought—I dreamed—you—"

"I'm not a dream," B.J. said.

"Don't—go."

"Not much chance of that," B.J. said grimly.

"Glad," Nola said, and then she slipped away.

B.J. hoped Nola had fallen asleep, but she knew this was not the case, and now she had a new, greater fear. Miles apart, her link to Nola had been strong enough so that she had been dragged down into the undertow when Nola lost consciousness. Here, so close, physically as well as psychically, the pull would be even stronger.

Gotta fight it, she told herself.

Think of Denny. She wanted to see him grow into a smart-mouthed teenager, an independent, sweet-natured man, to fall in love and have children of his own.

And Mama. She had always felt like just another compartment of her mother's life. She had accepted this. Now she realized that she wanted to be close to Iris, and she would, by God, live to do it.

There was Ward Trager, too, and the possibility of something between them.

And Nola. This peculiar bonding, this closeness—had it only happened because of the extraordinary situation? She wanted to know, and to do that she had to make up her mind to survive.

I'm not going to die down here, B.J. told herself, I'm sure as hell not going to die.

= 28 =

Ward woke suddenly, his senses tingling, his body soaked in sweat. Insects chirred in the jungle darkness. Knife points of stars pressed down. Night was no protection. They took special delight in coming when you were asleep, knowing you were particularly vulnerable when your body had finally surrendered. He thought that was why they took Remy so often. The poor bastard slept too easily.

Footsteps whispered on the grass. A hand gripped his shoulder, but it wasn't Charlie. It was his father, hunkering down beside the lawn chaise.

"Son, you can't spend the rest of your life like this. I know you had a terrible experience, but you can't give in. You got to fight it. Come on, now, your mom's all upset. She fixed up your room, bought you a brand-new mattress and everything."

"You gotta *try,* Mr. Trager." Denny stood on the other side of the chaise. "*I* would. I'd do *something.*"

"Sorry, Denny," he muttered and came fully awake.

The Merinos stared at him from the other side of the chain-link fence. He could smell their sheepy odor. His stomach roiled, and he tasted bile-flavored whiskey. When he squinted skyward, the stars whirled in bright eddies. He fumbled for the bottle, shook it, and heard a sloshing sound.

You had enough to drink, old sod.

Maybe, but it was a helluva long time till sunrise.

He took another pull of bourbon. His shoulders ached from the hard ground. Even the inside of the sleeping bag was damp from the dewfall. If he were home, out on the lawnchair, he thought he might go inside for a while and sleep on that new mattress beneath crisp clean sheets.

But he wasn't home—shit, mom and dad were not even home in that suburban Chicago house where he grew up. They had moved to Sarasota, Florida, five years ago. And the mattress probably went to Goodwill long before that.

When he called them now, they said, "We pray for you, son." They had stopped hoping. Seventeen years was a long time to hope.

A lone truck chugged by the Crossroads, headlights lancing the dark. Starshine reflected off glassy patches of black asphalt in the parking lot. The enclosure was shadowed by the overhang of roof, so he couldn't see the animal cages. The wolf run was empty. Lobo had not been out there at all tonight. Maybe the son of a bitch had finally curled up and died. Ward hoped he had, but he knew better.

Even at this distance, even in the darkness, he knew the wolf was watching him with those crazy, pleading, accusing, white-ringed eyes.

Gotta promise, Trag. Gotta make a pact. One of us can't stand it no more, the other finds a way. . . .

Remy—screaming in the cages, moaning in the communal cell, and when he couldn't scream anymore, his eyes saying, *do it do it do it.*

Ward had thought about it. He thought of little else. Since he could barely make a fist, there was no hope of putting his hands around Remy's neck and squeezing the life out. A gag, he considered that, and then pinching the nostrils closed. Remy would fight, though, and thrash about, alerting the guards. A bamboo splinter driven up the nose and into the brain—another discarded plan.

Oh, Ward thought of lots of things, but he didn't do any of them. It was too much to ask. *I never promised you anything, Remy. I never did.*

Remy starved himself eventually. Ribs like cattle-bones. That shrunken-skull face. And always the eyes . . .

Ward drank the last of the bourbon, every drop, and heaved the bottle into the brush. He stood up and walked unsteadily down the fence to the zoo. There was a ring of keys hanging on a nail to the right of the cages. As Ward unhooked the keys, he felt the wolf's stare and saw a prick of moonlight in its eyes.

(always the eyes)

"You're not gonna put it on me this time," Ward said. "By God, you're not."

He unlocked an outside gate to the run and left it standing wide. The inside door to the cage was already open. Now it was a straight shot for the wolf to the field, the trees, the wild stretches along the river.

The wolf never moved.

"Go on. Get."

Ward banged on the cage with his fist. He heard soft shuffling noises from the rattlers, a skittering of tarantula feet. The wolf didn't stir.

"Well, then, fuck you, Remy."

Ward stumbled back to his sleeping bag at the end of the pasture, wondering how he was going to get through the night without another drink.

B.J.'s eyes ached from the strain of trying to see in the blackness of the cellar. She could make out vague out-lines of the junk that had been stored down here—the old porch swing, scrap lumber, some paint cans, the benches.

The cellar was small to begin with, about five feet by

five feet of open space, and there was little room to move around. She hated sitting on the dirt floor and hated having Nola lie there. She didn't think she was strong enough to lift Nola up on the benches, however, and, anyway, she didn't relish the idea of sitting all crouched over because of the low ceiling.

Instead, she righted the swing, the motion starting fresh pain in her arm. She clenched her teeth, waiting for it to subside. When it settled to a dull pulse, she pulled Nola up to lie beside her with Nola's head in her lap.

Nola cried out. "Daddy? Aunt Vee?"

"No, I'm sorry. It's me."

"Annie?"

"Yes. Well, that's the name you had for me when I was a baby. It's really B.J. I saw your Aunt Verna when I went looking for you."

"Aunt Vee—" Nola tried to sit up and collapsed again. She radiated alarm, horror, despair.

"Please, just lie still," B.J. said. "Your aunt was all right. I'm sure she'll suspect something's wrong soon and come looking for you."

Well, Verna might, eventually, when she came out of her drugged fog, but from the looks of things she depended heavily on Frank. And what was the story there? Was he a relative? Friend of the family?

Nola murmured deliriously, and B.J. stroked her hair, trying to soothe her.

Nola wasn't coherent enough to be questioned, but B.J. had a pretty good idea what had happened to her. Nola must have stopped out here on her way to the airport. Maybe Frank was already here, or maybe he followed her. B.J. could imagine him coming on to Nola and Nola laughing in his slimy face. Or perhaps he just struck with brutal surprise.

Remembering the feel of his eyes on her body back there at the Douglas house, she thought his attack on Nola had to be a sexual assault. Had he actually raped Nola? Or did he get his thrills from the pain he inflicted?

Understanding the situation might not help, but it sure couldn't hurt. For one thing she'd simply like to know what she'd stumbled into. What she might even die for.

No, don't think like that. Come daylight she'd look for some way to get them out of this cellar. Meanwhile, surely Mama would worry. She'd made B.J. promise to call. Well, there were no phones down here in this hole in the ground. When Mama didn't hear, she'd never admit there might be a problem with her daughter's mental state, but maybe she'd get jittery thinking about the headaches and B.J.'s injured arm.

Jittery enough to call the police and ask them to look for her? *Mama?*

B.J. heard a soft scurry of movement under the bench. The sound seemed to crawl up her back on algid feet. The cellar must have stood empty for years. God knows what had taken up residence.

Nola heard the sound, too. She mumbled, "Dark things . . ."

B.J. could feel Nola drifting further and further away. And she could feel the tug of that downward slide, like an anchor hung around her own neck. She knew the two of them were linked. The question was, would she be dragged down into that deep, lightless sleep with Nola? Or would she hold Nola up, like keeping a lifeless swimmer afloat to prevent her from drowning?

More secretive movement under the bench. If she sank into that shared stupor with Nola, nothing would prevent whatever was under there

(dark things)

from creeping out.

She shook Nola. "Hey, wake up. Stay with me here. Nola?"

Nola's *yes* was more like a sigh.

"Did you remember me, or were you just as weirded out as I was by this stuff?" B.J. asked. "I could hear you in my head, calling me. Of course, I had no idea who Annie was. My mom told the story."

She repeated Iris's account of that time in the old house just after she was born.

"Talk about bonding," B.J. said. "Then there was this invisible friend I had when I was little. I'll bet you had one of those, too, didn't you?"

"Yes," Nola whispered.

"Well, hello, friend," B.J. said, feeling her voice catch in her throat. "You know, these past weeks I really did think I was losing my mind. Nice to know I'm not crazy—exactly—although I don't think many people would agree if I tell them about this."

If I live to tell them . . .

"I wish I knew how you got yourself into this." And how we're going to get ourselves out.

Nola whimpered and murmured something. B.J. had to lean close to hear.

"Water . . ."

"I'm sorry. I know you're probably still thirsty—"

"Flood," Nola said. "It's coming."

Nola had said the same thing before. B.J. thought this was probably her description of that feeling they shared, of sinking into a dark, watery grave.

"I've got you," B.J. said. "You just hang on to me."

But she was incredibly tired. And the pain in her arm was persistent as a toothache, draining her. It would be so easy just to close her eyes and drift. . . .

No, screw that. Keep your eyes open, she told herself. Keep talking.

"Nola, do you have any kids? I have a son. His name is Denny. . . ."

29

The Banty rooster chose the closest fencepost to sit and crow the sun up. Ward groaned. The shrill cry was like a spike driven into his right temple. He fumbled for a clod of dirt and heaved it at the rooster, who fluttered to the ground squawking loudly.

The first blinding rays of sunlight poked through the trees, driving the spike deeper. "Shit," Ward mumbled, eyeing the empty bottle. He couldn't imagine standing up, and the thought of walking . . . He managed both with grim determination, using the fence for a guide line.

Approaching the enclosure, he saw the open gate to the wolf run, and stopped, his heart beating raggedly. He had really done it. Lobo should have escaped, gone off to catch his own muskrat or raid some chicken coop.

But the wolf still crouched in the cage, too far gone to take his freedom when it was offered. There was nothing left of him but dull pelt over bare bones. And the eyes, of course. Always the eyes.

Ward closed the gate and locked it.

Shivering in the makeshift shower, he thought how nice it would be to bathe in hot water, to dry on fresh, fluffy towels. Getting soft, Trager? Or just getting tired? He thought it was all mixed up with the boy, Denny, and B.J. He'd started to see possibilities that delighted him and scared the hell out of him, all at the same time.

A family, a home . . . even if he admitted he wanted these things, stability required a steady job and money. He could see how a job application would read. *Work experience: baling hay, picking cucumbers, washing dishes, shoveling sheep shit.*

He could always go down to Sarasota and asked his folks for help, but he wasn't ready to do that just yet. Kindling hope was too much of a commitment, especially when he wasn't sure he really could work his way back into the mainstream or even if such a thing was possible.

Son, you got to fight.

Perhaps his dad had called it way back when Ward first got out of the VA hospital. Was it merely a lack of willpower that had kept Ward adrift? Suppose a person's store of willpower was like a battery, and all those years as a POW had drained him dry. Maybe it had simply taken the past seventeen years to recharge.

By the time he was dressed, Jerry had arrived and Ward could smell coffee brewing.

"Jesus," Jerry said, "you look like warmed-over shit."

Which just about summed up the way Ward felt. He washed down four aspirin with the coffee and waited for his stomach to decide what to do with it. When that stayed down, he went back outside, not even wanting to smell the bacon Jerry put on the grill, much less eat any of it.

The sun was up, riding the treetops, the air already heavy with heat and humidity. He saw Raylene arrive just ahead of two waitresses, and then early customers began to trickle in.

As he spread fresh hay and filled the water trough, he thought about Denny and B.J. again. Maybe she really had abandoned her son. Regardless of the rotten things Ward knew were happening all the time, he didn't believe she had. There was a special love between those two. If she'd left, she must have had a good reason.

Something to do with that incident in the kitchen. The idea popped into Ward's head without volition. He was probably dead wrong. He didn't have a clue to what had plunged B.J. into such severe shock, but he remembered the look on her face as she stood there with blood running down her arm.

"Something happened—" she had said. "To *her*. It happened to her."

He still didn't know what that was all about, but remembering the words sent an uneasy ripple up his spine. He had a good sixth sense for danger, developed on patrols in Nam where heeding that chill of premonition meant staying alive. Something's wrong, he thought, and just then Iris Johnson's old Dodge turned in off the highway.

She parked in front of the zoo and got out of her car. "Mr. Trager?" She hurried toward him. "Have you seen Denny?"

"No, I haven't. What's wrong?"

"He's gone. Run away."

She clutched the enclosure gate, sagging against it. Her lacquered hair was lopsided, molded by sleep. She wore old pilled polyester slacks and a pullover top. Her bare feet were thrust into tennis shoes.

"You're sure?" Ward asked.

She nodded. "I looked everywhere. The park. Up and down all the streets. I thought—somehow—he's so crazy about the animals here—"

She looked as though she might fly into a million pieces. There was an old wooden straight chair inside the enclosure. Moving quickly, Ward picked it up and took it outside.

"Here. You'd better sit down."

"No—I should go over to the café—" In the midst of protesting she sank down on the chair. "Maybe Raylene or one of the girls—"

"I don't think he came here, Mrs. Johnson. I'm sure I'd have seen him."

"That boy. As if I'm not worried enough—now this," she said. "I guess I shouldn't be surprised, the way he's been raised, dragged around from pillar to post. By the time I get home, he'll probably come strolling in acting like nothing happened."

"He might, but—" He could drop it right there and back away. Decide, he told himself and said, "When I saw him yesterday, he was pretty upset. He thinks his mother may have deserted him."

"What? Why, that's ridiculous. Whatever put such a crazy idea in his head?" She eyed Ward with her old suspicion that said, *I wouldn't put it past you to do something like that.*

"I told him I was sure he was wrong, but he was listening to his feelings, not to reason, Mrs. Johnson. Did he talk to you about it last night?"

"No—not exactly. Of course, we talked. He asked a million questions. I told him B.J. just went off to check on this—this person we used to know. That she'd probably be back last night or she'd call. . . . "

"But she didn't call, did she?" Ward guessed.

Iris jumped up. "She will today, and I ought to be there when she does. Denny'll turn up. I know he will. But if he should come here—I'd just as soon not talk to Raylene about this. Could you ask Al to call me?"

"Sure." He hesitated, then followed her to the Dodge. "Mrs. Johnson? This friend B.J. went to help—"

"Not a friend," Iris said. "Somebody—from a long time ago."

"Denny said B.J. went to Arkansas. Where in Arkansas?"

"That's no concern of yours." Iris fumbled for the door latch. Then, abruptly, added, "It's Chester. Chester, Arkansas," as she got in and slammed the door.

Watching Iris drive away, Ward knew Denny wouldn't be showing up here, and he wouldn't be at his grandmother's house in Dyersburg when she got home. Denny was more than worried about his mother, he was terrified. And he had not yet learned to accept the fact that he might be powerless to help her.

If you really wanted to—you'd try. I would. I'd do something—

Ward could feel the wolf's eyes on him. *Yeah, Denny would, Trag. Of course, on the way he might get run down by a semi or picked up by some helpful guy who really digs little boys, but he'd try.*

Ward locked the enclosure gate and strode quickly across the parking lot to the Crossroads' back door. In the kitchen flipping pancakes, Jerry glared at him balefully, sweat running in rivulets down his face.

"I need to use the pickup," Ward said.

"Raylene never said nothing." But Jerry jerked his head toward a pegboard where the key ring hung.

"Tell Al that Denny Johnson ran away, and I think I know where to find him."

"It's your ass." Jerry slapped pancakes on a plate, piled on sausages, and sailed the plate up on the counter, bawling, "Order up!"

Ward kept the Chevy Luv at a steady 52 mph as he headed for the river. At 53 the old pickup had a shimmy that would dance you right off the road. He had no doubt which way Denny was heading. The I-55 bridge crossed the Mississippi just south of Carthersville, Missouri. There was no other bridge until you got to West Memphis. With all the traveling Denny and his mother had done, the boy was sure to know that.

Ward hoped there was a road map someplace in the incredible jumble Al had piled in the glove box. King of the Road Trager—he knew a fair amount about the major highways himself, but he had never heard of Chester and figured it was some little burg off in the boonies.

Come to think of it, he'd bet Denny looked it up before

he left Iris's. He was a smart kid, and he would pick the shortest route, assuming he didn't get a lift from some kindhearted soul who was taking the long way around. And pray God it *was* a kindhearted soul and not some human piranha cruising for breakfast.

As Ward rumbled across the big arching bridge, he noted with dismay the narrowness of the breakdown lane and pictured Denny walking there. He squinted at the bright sunlight, his head throbbing. He'd picked a hell of a time to get drunk.

Once over the river he took the first exit. He was in the Missouri bootheel and only a few miles from the Arkansas border. There was a stop sign and then the road either went right into Carthersville or left into the countryside.

He pulled onto the gravel shoulder, stopped, and was leaning over to pop open the glove box for a map when he glanced to the left, and there was Denny standing along the road in the shade of the bridge.

Denny saw the truck turn and stuck his thumb out. He didn't recognize the pickup—he certainly wasn't expecting Ward—and he was already reaching for the door before he realized who was driving. He backed off and started walking, jaw set in a stubborn line.

"Denny—" Ward rolled along beside him. "Denny, come on and get in."

"No way," Denny said.

"Denny—"

A car flew past, inches away, honking indignantly.

"My mom's in trouble. I'm gonna find her, and nobody's gonna stop me."

"All right. Just for crissake get in the truck, and we'll both go look for her."

Something in Ward's face convinced him. Denny scrambled into the pickup. "You really are gonna help me look for Mom." There was wonder and relief in the boy's eyes. "Thanks, Mr. Trager. Thanks a lot."

Ward got busy monitoring the mirror and pulling back

out on the road. There was a curious expansion in his chest that reminded him of winter ice cracking on a mountain lake in the first warmth of an April sun.

"You're welcome, Denny," he said. "Now, I hope you know where Chester is, because I don't."

"I sure do. I looked it up on the map."

=== 30 ===

I'm so happy you're not a ghost," Nola said. "I'm so happy you came to find me."

She and Annie were walking along the riverbank. She was holding the little girl's hand. She was six herself, a lot bigger than her friend. A huge black panther followed them, insubstantial as smoke.

"Oh, Nola, I thought you understood," Annie said. "It was all a game. I just wanted you to feel better, so I said I was real."

As she spoke, her face softened, blurred, blew apart in the river breeze.

"No," Nola said, panicked. "No, you said so. You told me—"

Desperately, she clung to Annie's hand, but it dissolved like mist. For a moment she could see the hazy forms of Annie and the panther, floating in the air, and then they were gone. . . .

"Annie," Nola cried hoarsely.

She came out of the dream to total darkness, but her panic quickly subsided. She wasn't alone. Her head and shoulders rested against a warm breast. She could hear a heartbeat, faint but steady, beneath her ear and smell the sleeping woman's salty, pleasant scent.

Annie . . . No, not Annie, her little ghost child. B.J., Bethany Jean Johnson, real and alive, summoned by her own longing and the love of the child she once was.

B.J. had talked for a long time through the night. Drifting in and out, Nola missed a lot of what she said. But she had heard enough to know she was very glad that it was B.J. who had come to her. If anybody could get them out of here, she believed B.J. could.

But what if she couldn't? What if Frank came back, or—worse—left them here to die in the cellar? She might have called B.J. to her death.

Oh, Annie, she thought. What have I done?

By the time Frank told Verna what had happened the night before, she was quivering like a scared rabbit, coffee cup shaking so badly she had to put it down. He had waited for her to eat breakfast to give her the news. Now he wondered if that was a mistake, if she would upchuck into the toast crumbs.

"Oh, my God," she said. "Oh, my sweet Lord Jesus."

She wheezed harshly, and he could see a pulse thumping in her temple. He could always resort to Valium, but damn it all, he needed her help.

"Verna, you've got to calm down," he said. "Take a couple of deep breaths."

She obeyed, sucking in long gulps of air.

"Okay," he said. "That's better. Now, first of all, sweetheart, everything's under control. Remember that."

She nodded. She was still in the pink-flowered muumuu. She had been too groggy to change for bed the night before and hadn't showered yet, so she smelled of sour sweat. To Frank this was a considerable improvement over her usual dousing of sickeningly sweet bath powder.

"I've had time to think," he said. "And I know what

needs to be done. But I can't do this all by myself." He reached over and clasped her hands in both of his. "You have to be strong now, Verna. For us."

"What do you want me to do?" Her skin still looked mottled, blotches of red against pale white, but she was more controlled.

He released her with a little pat. "Well, the main thing, of course, is to get that other girl off the island."

"Who is she, Frank? Nola moved away when she was eight. I'm sure she didn't have any friends around here."

"She left her purse in the pickup, so I got a look at her driver's license. Her name's Bethany Jean Johnson."

Verna thought for a second, perplexed. "Sounds familiar, but—" She shook her head. "Why was she looking for Nola?"

"I don't know, but don't worry. I intend to ask her." Nicely at first. Then not so nicely if she refused to talk.

"You still didn't say what you want me to do," Verna said.

"Just drive me out to the island. I'll get Miss Bethany Jean, put her in her truck, and take her away. You come on back home. Then later all you have to do is come get me. I'll tell you where."

That wasn't all he intended for Verna to do. He had decided that if things went wrong she would be a lot more likely to keep her mouth shut if she were more directly involved in her niece's death. But there was time enough for her to find that out.

"What about Nola?" Verna asked.

"Oh, I doubt she made it through the night." Another lie. With the other girl there, he thought Nola might still be alive. In fact, he hoped she was. "We just take this one step at a time, and everything'll be all right. You'll see. Now why don't you go upstairs and wash up so we can get going."

"Okay." She got to her feet. "I was supposed to call Mr. Lasker this morning and let him know about the

176

offer, but I don't think I can do it, Frank." There was a reedy note of panic in her voice.

"Sure you can."

"But what should I tell him?"

"The truth. You called Nola and left messages, but she hasn't called you back."

He picked up the phone and handed it to her. She gulped air like a landed trout as she took the receiver and dialed. She managed the conversation with Lasker okay, but after she said goodbye, she let the phone slip from her sweat-slicked fingers, sending the receiver clattering against the tiled counter, reaching for Frank. He avoided her grasp long enough to hang up the phone.

"I don't like this, Frank. Oh God, please, don't let anything go wrong."

"Now, now, Verna." He suffered her moist weight as she clung to him and thought of fire again, of the old house on Painter's Island ablaze, of Verna's doughy body melting in the fierce heat like lard being rendered from a fat sow.

"Don't you worry," he said. "I promise you. I'm going to take care of everything."

"B.J.? B.J.?"

B.J.'s head rang with the frantic voice—both from inside and outside. "Okay," she said thickly. "Okay."

She opened her eyes to find herself slumped over Nola in the swing. In her lap Nola stared up at her, awake and alive. It took a minute to register the fact that the darkness had retreated—not a lot, but at least it was no longer pitch black. Alarm clamored somewhere in her brain, but her senses were dulled by that terrible lethargy that was nearly coma. All her efforts to stay awake had failed and, once asleep, she had become too closely linked with Nola.

"Denny," Nola said faintly. "You promised—"

"Yeah, don't worry. You'll get to meet him."

By sheer force of will she lifted Nola and slipped out, leaving Nola in the swing. B.J.'s shoulder muscles screamed in protest, and a flash of pain burned up her arm. One leg had fallen asleep, and it prickled as she put weight on it.

"Okay?" Nola asked.

"Fine. Great. Well, not great. Actually, I feel like shit, but we made it through the night. That's the important thing."

And, as far as B.J. could remember, the things under the benches had stayed away. She bent close to peer at Nola. She couldn't see well enough to assess how far Nola's condition had deteriorated, but she could guess.

"Have to tell you," Nola said, "about Aunt Vee . . ." But she was already slipping away.

"Hold on, you hear me?" B.J. squeezed her hand. "I'm going to find a way out of here."

She stood up, unsteady, her calves flaccid. Even in a crouched position, her hair brushed the low ceiling as she went up the steps and pushed against the door. It creaked open only a quarter of an inch, but she could see morning sunshine and a little of the deserted yard.

Still fighting the weakness that had turned her legs to jelly, she began exploring the planked ceiling, straining to see in the thick gloom, ducking away from the fine falls of dirt that seeped between the cracks. As she moved, sensation crept back painfully into her body. She hadn't eaten since lunch the day before. The last thing she had to drink was the can of Dr Pepper at the Conoco station. She preferred hunger and thirst over the awful numbness that Nola was feeling. And there was nothing like a good dose of panic to get the adrenals working.

"Nola? You still with me?"

Nola didn't answer—not out loud, but B.J. could feel her reply—something like a radar ping.

"I told you how my mom said Ward Trager gave her the willies. Wonder what she'd think about Frank? The guy reminds me of a snake, you know, or—"

Crocodile.

The word just there in her brain. "Yes. That's it exactly. He'll be coming back. We have to listen for his car."

He did not drive in last night, but then he had been sneaking up on them. Today he wouldn't have to bother.

"Let me know if you hear something."

If they could hear anything through the two feet of earth piled on the cellar. *If* he was planning to come back at all. . . . With each impenetrable inch of the sturdy wood ceiling that she examined, her panic grew. Maybe he was going to leave them locked in here. How long could you live without water? How soon until the things she heard scurrying along the edges of the cellar last night became bold enough to come crawling over her and nibble her flesh?

"Screw that," she mumbled.

Whatever she'd heard—rats, mice—they hadn't evolved in here. If they came in and went out, so could she. Oh, yeah, she thought, but you're not quite the size of a mouse—

Something swarmed out of a crack and ran up her arm. B.J. shrieked and brushed frantically.

"B.J.?" Nola cried.

"Shit—" B.J. shuddered, scrubbing at her shoulder and neck. "Don't worry—bugs of some kind. I'm all right."

Her skin still crawled, but she went back to the ceiling. God knows what else might lie waiting. She remembered another of Iris's stories, this one about B.J.'s great-great-grandmother, who lived in an old log house in the west Tennessee hills. During the day, timber rattlers liked to lie along the logs in the sun, and occasionally one would find a hole in the chinking and slither inside. . . .

179

Keep thinking like that and you'll be a screaming lunatic long before you die of thirst, she told herself grimly.

But B.J. couldn't keep the image out of her mind, and she kept remembering the soft shuffling sounds of last night and Nola's whisper, "Dark things."

═══ **31** ═══

Denny had the route memorized, so he and Ward found Chester all right. In town Denny hung out the window searching for the Toyota camper as they slowly cruised up and down the tree-canopied streets.

"She's gotta be here someplace," Denny said.

"Your grandmother never mentioned the name of this person B.J. came to see?"

Denny shook his head. "I shoulda asked her, but I knew she wouldn't tell me. Grandma never tells you anything. And I was afraid she'd figure out that I was gonna leave."

"Well, this is getting us nowhere."

They were back on the main street, which contained a row of buildings, most of them boarded up. The only ones still in operation were a café-bar called the Drop Inn, an all-purpose store that promised SUPPLIES, SUNDRIES, POST OFFICE, a tiny bank, and a Conoco station.

Not much to select from, so the gas station was the logical first choice, and, as luck would have it, the right one. A sullen kid, nursing a hangover, said, yeah, he remembered the camper and that the woman was asking the way to Miz Douglas's house. He didn't much like repeating the information, but he did, reluctantly.

With Denny navigating, they found the Douglas address easily enough, but there was no sign of B.J.'s truck. Although an old Pontiac sat on the driveway, nobody answered their repeated knocking.

Denny's shoulders slumped, and his eyes shone with unshed tears. "I'm getting really scared, Mr. Trager. We gotta find her. What are we gonna do?"

Ward might have suggested that they wait for the woman who lived here to return, but he had that jungle chill on his spine again. "Come on. Let's go find a telephone."

He tried Iris at home first. She snatched up the phone on the first ring.

"Denny?"

"It's Ward Trager, Mrs. Johnson. Denny's safe. He's here with me."

"Oh, thank God," Iris said. "Where are you? I'm going to skin that boy alive when he gets home."

"We're in Chester, looking for B.J. Has she called you?"

"No, she hasn't. I don't know what's gotten into that girl, worrying me like this." A hesitation. "Go find Verna Douglas, just ask anybody—that's where B.J. was going."

"We know that." He told her what they'd found at the Douglas place.

"Well, maybe B.J. left already. Maybe she's on her way home, and you missed her."

"Could be," Ward said. "But I don't think I'm going to get Denny away from here until we know for sure. Is there anyplace else she might have gone?"

"No—well . . . there is one place, but I can't imagine why she'd go there."

"What place?"

"This island, over on the Mississippi . . ."

* * *

B.J. slowly worked her way over the planked ceiling. She encountered a few more ants and an enormous, wooly centipede, enough to keep her mouth dry and her heart knocking.

To examine the bottom of the walls she had to kneel on the bench that ran around the three sides of the cellar. By the time she had worked her way into a corner, her eyes were adjusted to the low light, and she saw the wider crack between the boards. Her fingertips confirmed the difference—a good two inches of dirt, and the board below had a soft, cheesy feel. Lunch for those creepy-crawlies maybe, God bless them. She gouged out soil, grabbed the rotting board, and pulled a hunk free.

"Hey, I think I'm on to something." She scrambled off the bench, went back, and knelt beside Nola. "Nola? You hear me?"

No reply. B.J. had been so intent on finding an escape route, she had let the connection go. B.J. shook her. "Nola? Damn it, don't you slip away now. Answer me."

A faint, "Yes."

"Okay. You stay with me. I need something—"

B.J. looked through the pile of debris, salvaging a loose wood slat from the porch swing, a nail, and a bigger piece of old lumber.

In the corner she worked furiously, ignoring her injured arm and the fresh pain as a shard of wood burrowed into her palm. She dug away enough dirt, using first the nail and then the slat, so she could pry at the rotting board. A chunk fell out, causing a small avalanche as soil poured in. She let it cascade past her.

Once the worm-eaten board was pried free, she went to work on an adjacent piece, wedging the old lumber under and pushing against it. She was sweating now in the close, musty air, using up precious body fluids. Her arm throbbed violently. Blood seeped from the bandage and dripped off her elbow.

She felt the ceiling board loosen, but then the one she was using as a lever snapped. She had to work the remaining broken piece back in place. She beat on it with her fist, heaved—and the second board gave. More dirt poured in.

"Got it!" she sang out to Nola.

The next plank would be easier now that she had the second piece to use as a sturdy pry board. And once that was out, she could start digging through the earthen wall—

"*B.J.*," Nola called. "A car—"

B.J. froze and heard the sound of an engine, faint, but growing steadily louder.

Heart pounding, B.J. went up to the cellar door and crouched there, listening. An hour—that was all she had needed. In an hour she could have dug halfway to China. The car pulled up nearby and stopped. She cracked the door, but couldn't see the car.

Maybe it wasn't Frank after all. But she'd bet it was. She knew it was. Outside, car doors slammed. *Doors.* Maybe—*maybe*—a chance that somebody else had come instead of Frank, but she dared not rely on it. She needed a weapon. The board from the ceiling would do. If only there was someplace to hide at the entryway so that she could surprise him. Well, there wasn't. But if she could make him come down inside the cellar . . .

She plotted positions, put the board where it would be at hand, and went to lie on the floor beside the swing where Nola lay.

"B.J.? Is it—?"

"Shh, be quiet. I want him to think—"

B.J. blinked, squinted, blinded by the flood of light as the door flew open. She could make out the figure in the door and knew it wasn't Frank.

"Thank God," she said, flooded with relief as she recognized Nola's aunt.

"Nooo," Nola moaned and plucked at B.J.'s sleeve.

"It's all right." B.J. got up, saying, "Miss Douglas, I'm so glad—"

She broke off as Frank moved into view behind Verna.

She thought, Dear God, Verna's guessed what Frank has done and now he's kidnapped her too.

But then Verna turned away and let him take her place in the doorway. The gun in his hand pointed at them, not Verna. Nola knew, B.J. thought, sickened. She knew her Aunt Verna and Frank were in this together.

"Looks like we got here just in time," Frank said.

With the light shining in, B.J. could see that her clothes were filthy. Dirt coated her arms, mixed with blood on the one that had been injured. Her nails were black with grime.

"Bring Nola and come on up out of there," Frank ordered.

"I can't," B.J. said. "I'm exhausted. My arm hurts too much. I just can't do it alone."

"Fine," Frank said coldly. "Then you come up and leave her down there."

Grab the board—a paint bucket—or a handful of dirt to throw in his face. No, too late. If she made a move, he would use the gun. Like shooting fish in a barrel. She bent to lift her friend. Nola groaned, then wailed in pain.

"I'm sorry." B.J. felt tears burn the back of her throat. "So sorry."

"Hurry it up," Frank said. "And don't do anything stupid. Understand?"

B.J. pulled Nola to the steps and looked up. "I understand you're a fucking creep." She dragged Nola up toward the door. "What about you, Miss Douglas?" Verna had moved out of sight, so B.J. shouted it. "Verna? This is your own flesh and blood here."

B.J.'s head was even with the opening now. Frank reached out and grabbed a fistful of her hair, yanked savagely, drawing her head up and back. She gasped with pain, eyes watering, but somehow she remembered to hold on to Nola even as he tightened his grip and forced her to look up into his cruel, lightless eyes.

"You want to watch that smart mouth, girlie," he said softly and pressed the gun against her temple. "I may get tired of it real fast, and then I'll do something we'll both regret." He let go of her hair and stood up. "Out. Now."

Her scalp blazed with pain, and the muscles in her neck and back spasmed, but she managed to stagger up the last step and pull Nola with her out into the bright morning sun, where she collapsed in the long grass.

Frank grabbed her injured arm and yanked her up. She screamed in agony.

"B.J.," Nola cried. "Aunt Vee—"

"Please," B.J. said. "Let me stay with her. Please—"

"Frank, for God's *sake*," Verna said, hoarse and shaken.

"Verna, we talked about this. You know I'm only doing what has to be done. I put some rope in the car. Go get it and bring it in the house." To B.J. he said, "Move," and gave her a shove.

When she tried to resist, he dug in his fingers. She could feel the stitches tearing. Behind her Nola kept whimpering, "B.J. Annie . . ." but B.J. was no longer sure if Nola was really saying her name, or if Nola's voice was just there inside her head. She heard it over and over as Frank marched her through the rough, weedy yard, then up the steps of the high front porch.

He opened the front door and shoved her inside, sending her sprawling. Then he was on her, sitting astride her back, twisting her arm, shoving the gun against her neck.

"Verna," he yelled.

Through a haze of pain B.J. heard the woman's voice, edged with hysteria, and his, calm and flat. Nola was also there, in her head, calling and calling.

Frank grabbed the rope he asked Verna to bring. Verna refused to hold the gun, so he had to put the weapon down in order to have both hands free to tie B.J. up.

On her stomach with his weight pinning her there, B.J. went very still. Her head was turned toward the end table where he had placed the gun. She could see the ugly snout up there beneath a lamp hung with dull glass pendants. If she could get to it . . .

Frank wrapped the rope around the wrist of her injured arm and reached for her other wrist. No time left to think or plan.

She heaved and bucked, trying to throw him off. Caught off-guard, he let go her wrist, and she felt his weight shift as she wriggled and twisted.

Verna screamed. B.J. caught a glimpse of the woman, mouth rounded and hands over her ears. The noise she made was shrill yipping.

Frank bellowed, "Shut up and get outta here," and Verna bolted for the door.

Then he ended the struggle by yanking hard on the rope already attached to B.J.'s injured arm and simultaneously driving his fist into her breastbone.

Pain rocketed up to her brain and burst like shrapnel. A red haze bloomed. Through it, she saw Frank above her, his lank hair hanging in his sweaty face, a wild glint of glee in his eyes.

He bound her hands with the rope. Nothing she could do about it. Nola's calls were in her head again as he wrenched it tighter, and then . . . and then . . .

. . . and then Daddy threw her off the boat dock, and she smashed into the dark water, and it roared into her mouth and her ears and her nose and sucked her down, down to the thick mud and hidden rocks and the deep, black holes where dead panthers still roamed the earth. . . .

B.J. fought her way back to consciousness, knowing the vision was Nola's, but living it, too, churning the water, gasping for air. Opening her eyes, she saw she was alone on the floor in the living room of the old house. Frank was gone, but she knew where he was. She knew from the strength of her friend's terror that he was outside with Nola.

= 32 =

It's gotta be out here someplace," Denny said as they drove over the levee.

They had driven up and down the damn embankment a dozen times, following every dirt lane. Ward had never seen such a maze of dead ends. His head ached, and he longed for aspirin and strong black coffee.

Iris's vague directions had been of little help. "It's been twenty-six years," she had said. "You'll have to ask somebody."

"What am I? Fucking information?" The kid at the gas station had looked even meaner and surlier when they returned. "Never heard of the place."

But an older man in coveralls and a tractor cap, using one of the pumps, volunteered enough information to get them off the county blacktop. "Stop in at Sudder's," he had added. "They'll point you the way."

So far there had been no sign of the liquor-grocery store the man described. There hadn't been much of anything, just some empty buildings at the intersection when they left the county road and a few doomed-looking houses under dusty trees.

Denny hunched on the edge of his seat, peering out the window. "I don't know. Maybe we turned too soon."

"Maybe so," Ward said.

But then the road curved, and they could see the river, with sloughs cutting off chunks of land, forming a network of islands and sandbars.

Denny pointed and yelled, "Over there!" and Ward spotted the old, run-down store with its big metal sign reading LIQUORS, and a gray slat-thin hound lying on the narrow front porch.

Frank squatted on the ground next to Nola, happy to see that she was still alive. Her eyes were huge, sunken back in her head and glazed with fear.

"B.J.," she croaked. "Please—don't—"

"Oh, you got a lot more to worry about than your little friend, sister. A whole lot more."

Through the trees he could see Verna inching the Chevy Beretta out into the clearing. He stood up and waved encouragement. He'd had a few bad moments last night, thinking his plans were going down the tubes, but now everything was working out just fine.

One more little hump to get over with Verna, then he could dispose of little Miss Buttinsky Johnson. And for once he wasn't going to cheat himself. His mind was already humming with plans.

Verna parked the car and got out. She'd come downstairs from her shower earlier that morning in a blue dress, high-heeled sandals, and goddamn pantyhouse, for Christ's sake. He had sent her back to change into the gardening clothes she now wore: old pedal pushers, a chambray shirt, and a pair of splayed, dirty men's Adidas. She had big half-moons of sweat under her arms, and her face was damp and pink.

"That's all now, isn't it?" She carefully averted her face from Nola. "I can go on home."

"Not just yet."

Frank opened the door on the passenger side of the Chevy and bent over Nola. She tried to pull away, which was stupid since all she was doing was prolonging things and keeping him out in the blistering sun.

"Verna, give me a hand here."

"No," Verna said in revulsion. "I can't—no."

Better not argue on this one. He gave Nola's snake-bit arm a brutal squeeze and she went limp. He picked her up and dumped her inside the Chevy on the front seat.

Verna jumped at the sound of the door slamming shut. "Easy does it," he said, coming over to put his hand on her shoulder.

"This is taking too long," she said shrilly. "I want to go home now."

"It's almost over." He took out a handkerchief and mopped his face. "There's just one little change of plan we need to discuss, sweetheart."

She stared at him, eyes full of apprehension. "Change? What? You said you would take the car over the bridge—and then—the river and—"

"That's still going to happen. But I want you to drive the car instead of me."

"No!" She backed off, shaking her head. "No, Frank."

"Just listen, Verna. What we're doing here—all of this—it's for our future, for both of us. You know that. But the problem is, sweetheart, so far I've handled everything. I don't mind. I'd do anything for you. But I need to know you're in this with me, Verna."

She still shook her head, no, no.

"It's important," he said earnestly. "It's just like standing up in front of a minister and saying for better or worse. If you absolutely can't do it, well, I'll understand. But I think it'll be a wall between us, Verna. I really, truly do. And it's so easy."

She stood, mute, but now she wasn't saying no.

"Remember how I described what was going to happen?" he asked. "We want it to look like she got bitten by that snake, fell and hurt herself, but she managed to get to the car and tried to drive off. So—what you do, you just go right across the bridge. Then you head off the road and steer toward the river. You can see where I mean, can't you? Over there by the old boat dock?"

He put his arm around her quivering shoulders and pointed through the trees to the sandy hillock that sloped down to the water where a few old pilings stuck out like eroded teeth. She nodded reluctantly.

"When you get to that point, you stop. Then you make sure the brake's off and the car's in gear and get out. The car will just keep rolling. That's easy. Simple."

He turned her toward him, caught her face between his hands, and forced her to look at him. "You have to do this, sweetheart. If you want us to have any kind of future together, you have to do it."

She drew a long, shuddering breath, and nodded.

"Good girl," he said.

Nola's calls ricocheted inside B.J.'s skull, and her friend's pain and terror became as real as her own. She wrenched futilely at the ropes binding her arms. The rough fiber skinned the flesh from her wrist bones. Her hands felt warm and slippery from blood.

Her wrists were bound in front of her, then tied to her ankles. As a result, her knees were up between her arms right under her chin, and she was bowed into a ball. She might be able to get to the door, but, once there, she would never be able to stand.

Through sobs of agony and frustration, she heard an engine start up. They were leaving, taking Nola—

boat dock, no, daddy, pleasepleaseplease

She heard Nola's voice, her own voice, keening wildly.

Then Frank entered the room, grabbed her, and hauled her up to a sitting position. "Stop that damn racket." He shook her so hard her teeth clacked together. "You either quit carrying on, or I'll stuff something in your mouth." He untied her ankles and pulled her to her feet.

Kick him in the balls, B.J. thought, a knee under the chin . . .

The ideas came a fraction of a second too late, a precious lag of time, her brain working slowly because she was still hearing Nola's screams. And then he was gripping her injured arm, pushing her ahead of him, to the door.

"Bastard," she said. "Murdering goddamn bastard. Why? Why are you doing this?"

Opening the door, he turned toward her, wearing a toothy crocodile smile. "Why not?"

Then he hauled her around and thrust her out onto the porch, holding her there while he put his face right against hers so they were both looking out through the trees toward the pontoon bridge where they could glimpse Nola's rental Chevy moving slowly across with Verna at the wheel.

B.J. fought him, tried to twist away, but he gripped her tightly.

"Watch," he said. "You don't want to miss this."

"I don't want to," Daddy said. "God knows I don't, but it's the only way."

Only it wasn't Daddy saying the words, it was Aunt Vee, looming above her in the car, hunched over the steering wheel, all her softness turned to gargoyle angles. Aunt Vee, taking her to the boat dock.

"Please," Nola said. "Please—don't—"

"You think I like this?" Aunt Vee said. "I just hate doing it, but I've got no choice. I gave up my life for that old woman, and she lied to me. She let me think there was lots of money, and I would get it all. It's not right, what she did. It's not fair, not fair and—"

"Aunt Vee—"

"—and I just don't care anymore. I'm thinking of myself for once. Frank'll leave me if I don't have the money. I know he will. I want to get married. I want nice clothes and nice things and—"

Nola plucked feebly at her aunt's sleeve, but Verna rambled on, unheeding as they bumped off the pontoon bridge on to the road.

B.J. Annie . . .

But B.J. wouldn't come this time. Frank had her. And Frank had a gun. B.J. wasn't dead. Not yet. Nola could still feel her with her mind. But soon . . .

Aunt Vee turned the Chevy off the road. Maybe she would park now, tell Nola she was sorry, that of course she couldn't do anything to hurt her. Then Nola would persuade Aunt Vee to turn around and go back for B.J.

Her aunt's face looked raddled and old. She gripped the steering wheel with both hands and stared out the windshield as the car lurched slowly over the sandy soil.

Make sure the brake's off and the car's in gear. . . .

Nola had caught only bits and pieces of the conversation, but she knew Frank had said that and then something about the boat dock. And now Aunt Vee had turned off the road toward the dock. But that was crazy. The boat dock was gone, dismembered by a flood. Only a few stumps of pilings were left, slimy with oil spilled from the barges and rotted by the water. There was nothing ahead but

(Make sure the brake's off and the car's in gear)

the river . . .

Her heart expanded with horror. She remembered being three years old and flying through the air into the cold, dark water, how the water grabbed her ankles and sucked her down, down, down. . . .

Aunt Vee braked to a jerky stop. She leaned over, fumbled with her left hand to check the brake, and touched the gearshift with her right.

Nola's breath locked in her throat. She scrabbled, felt the fabric of Aunt Vee's shirt beneath her fingertips, and the soft flesh of her aunt's arm.

"Aunt Vee, no, please, no—"

Verna reached for the door handle. She took her foot off the brake. The car rolled forward slightly.

"Aunt *Veeeeee*," Nola screamed.

She dug her fingers into Verna's jellylike flesh, using both hands, trying to get a grip.

"Let go of me." Verna twisted frantically.

Nola felt Verna's arm slipping away. She locked her hands together, anchoring them around the knobby protrusion of Verna's wristbone.

The car moved a little faster.

"Damn you. Goddamn you." Verna beat at her. Her fist was like a club smashing at Nola's face.

Bone crunched in Nola's nose. Pinwheels of light exploded in her head, but she hung on. She felt the car gathering speed. Verna bleated in terror. She shook her captured arm, flopping Nola like a rag doll. She pried at Nola's fingers, then finally sank her teeth into Nola's wrist.

Nola screamed and let her go.

Too late for Verna.

The car left the sandy hillock with a weightless moment of flight and arched out toward the water.

33

Frank felt B.J. writhe in agony as she watched the car roll down the slope toward the river. She screamed and swore and thrashed around. She was strong for a woman, just about as tall as he was, and she had the added strength of fear and panic. He really couldn't pay a whole lot of attention to the action down on the riverbank and hold on to B.J. at the same time. Also, the view of the river from the porch was blocked by trees.

He wasn't sure exactly what tripped the little alarm in his brain, but he knew something wasn't right. Verna, he thought. Where the hell was Verna?

She wouldn't hang around up there watching the car go in the drink. No, she'd hightail it back to the road and the bridge, as fast as her plump legs would carry her. He ought to be seeing her now, even with the trees blocking the view.

And then Frank watched as the car left the ground, sailing out toward the water, and he saw Verna—it had to be her—in the car, the goddamn fucking car.

"Jesus Christ," he said. "Stupid *bitch*—"

Stunned, he slackened his hold on B.J. She wrenched

free and slammed an elbow into his stomach. His breath woofed out, and he doubled over. The gun flew from his nerveless fingers. Paralyzed with pain, all he could do was hold his stomach and lean against the porch rail for support, while B.J. yelled, "Nola! Nola!" and plunged down the steps.

With her hands bound, her balance was off, so she tripped and fell into the weeds. Pain was roaring in Frank's ears now, and red speckles danced in his eyes. He coughed, gagging, as he watched B.J. stagger to her feet. Clinging to the railing, he lurched onto the steps and whooped in air with a strange cawing sound.

B.J. was up. She stumbled across the yard and fell again. She was the one—ruined everything. Turned his careful plans into a royal fucking mess. Verna out there in the car, in the river. Was there any possibility of getting her out? Maybe. But he had to get B.J. first. Shoot the bitch. Make sure she didn't get away.

His gun . . .

He went back up to the porch. Not there—it had flown out of his hands. He remembered the sound of metal skating across wood. It must have gone off the porch, but which way?

He wanted to howl with frustration. He wanted, very much, to catch B.J. and throttle her with his bare hands, but there was no time, not if he wanted to get to Verna before she drowned.

He galloped down the steps—never mind the god-damn gun—and raced after B.J. He cast about for a weapon as he ran, something to smash the bitch's head in, saw a piece of scrap lumber and stopped to seize it; it was a good big piece pierced by a rusty nail. Then he was off and running again, thinking of Verna and B.J. and how to cut his losses.

That was when he caught the flash of sunlight on chrome through the trees and saw the old pickup coming across the pontoon bridge.

* * *

"There it is." Denny pointed to a house partially hidden by trees.

Ward sensed danger even before he saw it. That old patrol-sharpened warning raised the hair on his neck like quills.

Sunlight knifing through the trees. A glitter of rain on broad leaves, a cloying jungle stench. Their stench, the Cong. He could smell the little bastards. He waved frantically to Remy, to the snot-nosed lieutenant, but the idiots kept coming. His mind shrieked alarm. And then he saw them, running toward him—

"Mom!" Denny cried.

Ward stamped on the brakes, rocking to a stop. Around the curve he saw, not the Cong, but B.J. stumbling through the overgrown yard, and a man chasing her with a club in his hand.

Even before the truck came to a stop, Denny opened the door. Ward realized what he was doing and lunged for him—too late.

Plans ran through Ward's head with the speed of light. He had no weapons with him. There was probably a tire iron someplace in the truck. No time to get to it. All he had was the truck itself and his own body. He considered driving at the man and running him down, but it was already too late for that. Both Denny and B.J. were in the way, and, just to complicate things, there was a dusty black Buick along with B.J.'s camper parked near the house.

B.J. cried, "Denny—no!" She turned to intercept her son, stumbled, and fell.

Denny ran, knees pumping, yelling, "Get away! Leave her alone!"

He was going to end up between the man and his mother somewhere near the steps that went up to a high front porch, Ward could see that, and not a damn thing he could do except bolt from the truck and run as fast as his legs would take him.

The man with the club hadn't expected Ward or

Denny, and he may have hesitated for a few seconds, but not long enough, not nearly long enough. Ward knew he wasn't going to make it even as he saw the man change targets, charge toward Denny, and scoop him up.

He held Denny with his arm locked around the boy's chest, ignoring Denny's flailing legs and pummeling fists.

"Stop right there," he ordered, and Ward had no choice but to obey.

"Shithead," Denny yelled. "Asshole—let me go—" He broke off with a yelp as the man gave his chest a brutal squeeze.

"Denny—don't let him hurt Denny," B.J. screamed. She was filthy. Blood stained her tank top and covered her arms. Her wrists looked abraded and raw. She wept silently, tears running down her face. "Frank, please," she said to the man. "The car—they'll drown—"

Frank ignored her. His eyes were on Ward. "I told you, stay back."

"Right. Sure," Ward said.

Ward didn't try to approach the man, but he did step nearer to B.J., saying, "It's all right."

"No, no—the car—in the water—Nola—"

Ward had no idea what she was talking about, but he sensed the urgency. She wore that far-off look again, then she seemed to drag herself back and focus on Denny.

The boy whimpered in Frank's grasp. Scared now, but he still wriggled and fought. Frank watched Ward as his snake-flat eyes flickered around, searching for a way out.

Ward risked another sideways step toward B.J. "Frank? Why don't you stop this right now and put the boy down. You're a little shit, Frank. I've got half a foot and forty pounds on you, and I spent a couple of years in Nam killing with my bare hands."

"Back off," Frank said. "Think you're so tough. Let me tell you. I've had some practice, too. Maybe I can't kill this little fucker before you get to me. But I can do him some real damage."

Frank hefted the board with its big spike of rusty nail.

198

Ward could imagine it smashing into Denny's skull, his eye, his ear drum. Denny's eyes shone with terror.

Up on her knees now, B.J. shook her head and moaned in an eerie monotone, "Water—high waters—Daddy—"

Ward's heart hammered, but it was the old jungle beat, clearing his head and honing his senses. Everything was crisply focused, startlingly detailed. Keep moving. Keep sharp.

"Okay, Frank. I can see you're serious. What do you want? Talk to me."

"I just want out of here," Frank said. "I want the car—"

"The Buick, right?"

"Yeah, the Buick." More looking around, a twitchy grasshopper gaze. "Once I'm inside it, I'll turn the boy loose."

Like hell, Ward thought. And what was Frank looking for? Not at his escape route to the car. Something in the grass, around the steps.

"He's lying, Mr. Trager," Denny said. "Don't let him—"

Frank gave the boy another squeeze.

"It's okay, Denny." Ward had good peripheral vision. Shit, to survive in Nam you had to have eyes in the back of your head. He didn't take his gaze off Frank, he just drifted to the right some more and used the edge of his sight . . . and saw a glint of sunlight off something metallic.

A gun.

"Go ahead," he said to Frank. "As long as you let the boy go, that's all I want."

Flashback, Ward thought, his chest tight because he was so goddamn afraid. He blinked. It was still there, a real gun—a by Christ real thirty-eight lying in the grass just two feet away.

Now I know what you're looking for, you bastard, Ward thought.

Frank hadn't seen the gun. But he hadn't moved either. Ward advanced a step toward him to give him a little incentive.

Frank made up his mind and retreated. The Buick was about a hundred feet away, the door to the driver's side facing Ward.

"What are you waiting for?" Ward said. "Christ, man, let's get this over with."

"Mr. Trager—" Fear bleached Denny's face.

"Denny, I want you to trust me. Do exactly what I say."

"Uh-uh—"

"Exactly, Denny. Understand? Now, go on with Frank and behave yourself."

"Denny—" B.J. cried.

She staggered to her feet as Frank backed away and began moving swiftly toward the Buick.

"Stay there," Ward ordered, motioning her to keep out of it.

"But—Denny—"

In a second she was going to dart after them. Ward moved swiftly and yanked her down.

"Goddammit, do what I say," he said.

Then he was up, urging Frank silently, *go on, go on,* calculating distance and time. Diving for the gun and praying that the safety was off and there were bullets in the chamber, praying that Denny would react, knowing there would be only one chance.

Frank did just what Ward thought he might do. He didn't release Denny. Instead, he opened the car door and threw the boy inside.

"Denny!" Ward yelled. "Get down. NOW!"

Denny wrenched free and dived for the floor. For one perfect moment Frank's head was a bull's-eye. Ward Trager—combat veteran, sharpshooter, ordinary man who by God wasn't ever again going to let anybody fuck up his life—that Ward Trager had him dead in his sights, and he blew the top of Frank's head off.

34

Daddy threw them off the boat dock. Nola floated down in an eternity of free-fall with Aunt Vee's shrieks dinning in her ears. Then they hit with a jarring thump and a tremendous splash.

But she wasn't wet. Of course not. She was in a *car,* not the water. This was another nightmare. A hallucination. Any minute she would open her eyes and she'd be back with B.J. No, this was some stupid scenario of Chuck's and she was reliving it in her dreams—in 70mm and Technicolor.

Nola opened her eyes.

The world was shrouded in a peculiar murky darkness, but she could see she was slumped on the seat in the Chevy Beretta beside her aunt. Verna's screams shrilled to a crazed pitch. Nola glimpsed her bulging eyes and rounded mouth as she pounded at the windows.

And outside the windows—not a dream, *water,* outside, all around, the silt-laden river, and then she felt it lapping at her ankles, climbing to her knees with horrifying speed, over the seat, over her head—

She clawed at Verna for support, pulled herself upright, sputtering, out of the water, but—oh God—not for long. It surged to her chin. *Flood. High waters.* No, they were in the river. Verna had steered the car into the river. She had planned to jump out, but Nola had grabbed her, and Verna was trapped too.

Verna bellowed louder and shoved Nola away. She churned wildly, splashing water into Nola's face and eyes. Nola coughed and choked. Her head rang with pain and the force of Verna's screams.

Get out. Door. Window. Acting on her thoughts was a different matter. Her motor functions seemed disconnected. It was all she could do to stay erect. Worse, her aunt floundered like some enormous, berserk fish. Verna's flailing arms battered at Nola, inflicting more pain, upsetting Nola's precarious balance.

Nola slid away toward the door, using it for support, while she ran her hand over the vinyl-covered panel, trying to find the handle. She realized suddenly that something had changed, but it took a moment to understand what it was. Just at the level of the dash, the water had stopped rising; at least she thought so, but it was almost impossible to tell because so little light penetrated the muddy river above them.

The water had compressed the air in the car. Yes, that made sense. The two elements had reached an equilibrium.

Aunt Vee's screams subsided to wild gibbering, so Nola heard the bubbling sound by the window. A faint little *pop pop* like blowing through a straw. Because, of course, the balance between air and liquid was only temporary. In the end, the water would win.

But then, she had always known it would.

B.J.'s head still rang with the shot Ward had fired. Beside the Buick, Frank's arms beat the air a couple of times, birdlike, then he dropped like a sack of flour down a chute, sliding feet first from beneath the open door to the ground. Blood splattered the windows, paint-bright.

Denny.

Fear for her son drove Nola's terrified calls from her mind for a moment. Ever since Frank had dragged Nola away, B.J. had felt split in half. She dimly remembered that Ward had shouted a command to Denny. She thought Ward had moved and used the gun with precision and care. Still, Denny was only inches away from the path of the bullet.

As she clumsily got to her feet, B.J.'s mind filled with images of lead fragments ricocheting off the metal surfaces of the car and ripping into Denny's body. . . .

She ran, staggered, caught herself, and kept going. Ward was already ahead of her, charging for the car, yelling Denny's name.

Before he reached the Buick, the door on the passenger side opened, and Denny tumbled out. He hit the ground running, came around the car, and leaped into Ward's arms.

Ward brought him back to her. Blood spattered her son's face, arms, and the front of his T-shirt, but Ward said quickly, "I don't think it's his."

"Are you sure? Denny—"

"I'm okay, Mom."

Ward still held him, but the boy leaned over to cling, monkeylike, to his mother.

"I'm glad you shot him, Mr. Trager," Denny said fiercely. "I hope he goes straight to hell."

"Easy with your mom," Ward said. "Let's get that rope off her wrists."

"Hurry—please," B.J. said.

Relief cleared the barrier that her fear for Denny had created, and Nola's frantic call came pouring in.

"She's still alive—in the water—"

Ward worked at the knots. "Who's alive?"

"Nola—God, she's so afraid—"

The knot came free. She did not take the time to explain. She just turned and ran for the pickup.

"Come *on!*" she cried.

To his credit, Ward didn't hesitate. He grabbed Denny, and they all piled into the truck.

Pop pop pop.

The air leaked away, faster and faster. Nola could see the little bubbles outside the top of the window, vanishing quickly into the silt-laden river.

The water level inside the car had risen to about a foot below the roof. The light seemed to have been forced out, too, as well as the air. Darkness descended, thick as soup. Outside the car she could see little except for a couple of pilings, the remnants of the old boat dock.

As the water crept closer, Nola drew on some remaining reserve of strength to push herself up on her knees. The water helped to buoy her up. Her stamina was vanishing at an alarming rate, however. She wasn't sure how long she would be able to keep her head above the water.

Verna's endurance was flagging too. She stopped pawing at the window and now scratched at the roof. Her nails tore through the fabric headliner and scraped metal, the sound making Nola shiver. Verna's head was tipped up near the roof, and she breathed in great shuddering gasps.

Nola thought that B.J. must be dead. That Frank had killed her. One moment B.J. had answered, and the next she was gone.

Without B.J. it was only a matter of time—until the air ran out, until the river claimed her.

Nola thought how easy it would be to stop fighting. The water plucked at her with gentle fingers. So easy to give in and let it pull her down. To lie on the seat and rest.

Screech screech—Verna's nails on the metal.

The water rose another inch, lapping at her mouth and filling her ears. Her head felt massive, as though the liquid had filled it to near-bursting.

I tried, Grandma. I really did.

She slid down into the water's embrace.

Nola? Nola?

B.J. calling to her.

Nola felt a dim elation and sent back a few last scattered thoughts. *So glad—wish, but—too late . . .*

B.J.'s message came pouring in. Not words exactly, but Nola understood all right. *We've come this far and I'm not going to let you give up, you hear me? Screw this resting shit. I won't stand for it, so you get yourself up and you breathe, goddamn you—*

—you keep breathing and you keep trying—Nola? NOLA?

B.J. sent her frantic signal as the pickup skidded to a halt at the top of the sandy hillock. She raced down the slope and into the river with Ward right behind her.

While concentrating on keeping a lifeline to Nola, she had managed only a few stilted words of explanation during the brief ride. No matter. Ward Trager was pretty damn fast on the uptake.

"You stay put," Ward yelled at Denny, his tone brooking no argument, as B.J. pointed to the area beside the boat dock.

The water was a dense gray-brown, but she could see the vague outline of Nola's car. B.J. took a deep breath and dived. She felt a faint response from Nola, so faint that her own heart pounded with urgency.

The Chevy was about ten feet down. Not far, but the visibility was so bad, it was like looking through sludgy coffee. Ward touched her arm and motioned. He'd take the driver's side and deal with Verna.

B.J. grabbed the Beretta's chromed molding, pulled herself down, and looked inside with her face right up against the window. The water in the car was about nine inches from the roof and rising rapidly. One head was above the water, but it was on the other side of the car—Verna.

Nola. NOLA!

Nola floated like a fetus in amniotic fluid, her hair

fanned out, suspended. B.J. tugged futiley at the door handle until the water filled the car. With the pressure equalized, the door opened.

She reached for Nola. Her own lungs burned, ready to burst. She ought to go up for air, but she knew she didn't dare. She was so tired now. She thought how nice it would be to stop for a while, to let the water cradle her . . .

Stop it, she told herself. Those were Nola's thoughts, not hers.

Dammit, Nola, we are not going to stop or rest or fucking drown. We are getting the hell out of here.

She grabbed Nola's shoulders, yanking hard but feeling her motions slowed by the water. She was dimly aware that Ward had the other door open, that he had his hands full with Verna, who had no idea she was being rescued and thrashed about in extreme panic.

B.J.'s chest was on fire now, her head whirling. If she didn't get air soon, she'd open her mouth by reflex and breathe in liquid.

Nola was free from the car, but she was a dead weight, and B.J. was exhausted. She could see Verna's head bobbing inside the car, but no sign of Ward.

And then she felt his arm slide around her waist. He moved between her and Nola, holding them both, adding his strong, powerful kicks to hers so that they arrowed up, swift and sure, through the dark water.

35

Once they got the water out of Nola's lungs and started her breathing again, everybody piled into B.J.'s camper, Ward driving, B.J., Nola, and Denny in back. Ward still didn't know what was going on between the two women, but, crazy as it seemed, he'd swear their reactions were somehow tied together. Nola was so deeply in shock she was barely alive. And Ward could see that same withdrawal from the world creeping into B.J.'s eyes.

"You keep a sharp watch," he told Denny. "And keep your mother talking. Anything funny, bang on the window."

"I sure will," Denny said. "Now let's go."

He'd already given Ward a quick rundown on the best route to Blytheville. He'd memorized that, too, he said proudly, from the map.

Driving as fast as the potholed dirt road would allow, Ward shivered in his wet clothes and turned on the heat. He flew past the liquor store where old Mr. Sudder stood on the porch staring off at the island. Maybe the man had heard the shot, suspected something was very wrong, and would either call the police or would go out himself to investigate. Ward wasn't going to stop and find out.

Time enough later to explain the two deaths—Frank with a bullet in his head, and Verna who must surely be dead too. Ward never saw her surface in the river. By the time he got B.J. and Nola ashore, cleared Nola's lungs, and applied mouth to mouth resuscitation, he knew it was useless to go back for Verna. She'd been down too long, and Nola needed immediate medical attention.

B.J. was in no condition for long explanations, but he did get the bare bones. Verna Douglas had tried to kill her niece. And Verna was at least an accomplice in planning B.J.'s murder.

When they finally reached asphalt, Ward pushed the Toyota up to a wallowing seventy, making only one brief stop at a gas station for directions to the hospital. In Emergency, while doctors attended to Nola and B.J., Ward called Iris collect. He couldn't answer her frantic questions because he didn't know the details himself. But he could tell her where they were and that her daughter and grandson were safe.

Ward waited with Denny until B.J. reappeared, her arm bandaged. She had let the doctor restitch her wound and treat her assorted cuts and bruises, but she adamantly refused to be admitted.

"You should be in bed, Miss Johnson," a nurse said. "It may be quite a while before we know anything for sure about your friend."

"No, I need to be with my family—" B.J. broke off, glancing at Ward, and amended, "I mean, with Denny."

But Ward knew that for a moment at least she had meant to include him. Denny caught it too. He looked from his mother to Ward, then got a big happy grin on his face and a look in his eye that said, oh ho, why didn't I think of that?

Ward was going to have to have a talk with the boy.

Yeah, lot of good that would do. He knew what Denny would say. You gotta *try.*

Well, maybe so. But it was a hell of a long way from

B.J.'s slip of the tongue to any kind of real relationship. Ward had known the two of them less than a week. He'd formed an instant bond with the boy, and he was attracted to B.J., but he'd never so much as kissed the woman, for crissake.

Then there was the little matter of being a dropout from the world for seventeen years, no decent job, no money—so why was this well of optimism bubbling up inside him?

"Please," B.J. said to the nurse, "as soon as you know anything about Nola—"

"I'll let you know," the nurse promised.

"If you've got some coffee, it would help," Ward said. "And maybe something for her to eat."

The receptionist produced cookies, orange juice for Denny, and coffee for the grownups.

B.J. sat with her arm around Denny, but her attention was on the room down the hall where Nola lay. B.J. looked haggard and pale, with that faraway detachment in her eyes.

"There may come a point when you have to decide," Ward said quietly. "You may have to let her go."

She glanced up, startled. "I know, but right now I can help her. I can't explain how—"

"You don't have to," Ward said.

Ward put his scarred hand over hers. She hesitated, then laced her fingers with his, hanging on. For once Denny was silent, content to sit there and sip his orange juice.

Ward had expected the cops to show up, so he wasn't surprised when two uniformed state policemen came in—a look-alike duo, with mustaches and mirrored sunglasses. They spoke to the receptionist and walked over, eyeing Ward, a cold and alert appraisal, hands hovering above their holsters. Ward had been rousted enough times to know they were already picking him as their prime suspect because of his rough appearance.

209

"Man's been killed," one of the cops said. Crawley, according to the little plastic I.D. tag on his shirt pocket. "Named Frank Moser. You people know about that?"

"I do," Ward said. "I shot him."

Guns leaped into their hands. "Up against the wall," Crawley said. "Move it."

"What are you doing?" Denny said indignantly.

B.J. chimed in with her protests, too, but the cops ignored them until they patted Ward down and took his wallet. At least he had a driver's license, wet but legitimate I.D.

"That Frank guy kidnapped my mom." Denny got right in the cop's face and wouldn't back off. "He grabbed me and put me in the car. He was gonna kill us. Mr. Trager saved our lives."

The patrolmen listened with practiced skepticism to B.J. as she told them how she found Nola and had been caught by Frank herself, how Denny and Ward had tracked her down and what had happened on the island.

Crawley chewed on the edge of his mustache and said to his partner, "What do you think?"

"You kidding? We got to take him in."

"Mom," Denny implored. "They can't put Mr. Trager in a cell and lock him up. Please, don't let them."

"For God's sake," B.J. said to Crawley. "Didn't you hear what I just told you?"

"We don't have a choice, ma'am," Crawley said.

From the look on Denny's face Ward didn't know if the boy was going to launch himself at the cop with fists flailing or burst into tears.

"I'll be all right, Denny," Ward said. "You just take care of your mom, okay?"

Denny flew to him, wrapped his arms around Ward's waist, and hugged him tightly. A bright burst of love flooded Ward's heart. Ward hugged the boy back and knew that, by God, they might be taking him to jail, but they wouldn't keep him there for long, because Denny and B.J. still needed him.

When the jail-cell door clanged shut behind him, Ward felt the old panic well up. He forced himself to go and sit on the hard bunk and consider his situation. The two patrolmen had treated him politely, even forgoing the handcuffs on the way in. For Denny and B.J.'s sake, Ward had taken care to be cooperative and curb any hostility, so the staff at the police station had been courteous, almost apologetic. He thought it was only a matter of time until he was released.

What bothered him was the amount of time involved, because he was okay now, he could deal with the confinement and keep his anxiety under control. The real test would be nightfall, when sleep lowered his defenses and the dreams arrived.

He jumped up and paced the narrow space. Ward was alone in the old jail except for a drunk snoring loudly in another of the four cells. A strong smell of disinfectant didn't hide the ancient jailhouse odors or the drunk's acetone stink. Through a high, small window Ward could see twilight purpling the sky.

Darkness fell, much more swiftly than usual it seemed to him, and yet he felt time creep slowly past. He had learned in the POW camp that prison keeps its own clock. Hours passed—or maybe it was only minutes—before the door to the jail block opened. Al Norris trailed a cop back to Ward's cell.

"Al?" Ward said, astonished.

"Come on, Trager," Al said. "Let's get you the hell outta here."

When Iris called the Crossroads to tell Al what had happened to B.J., she was so shaken, Al decided she was in no condition to drive. At the hospital they had learned about Ward's arrest, and Al had come right over.

According to Al, getting Ward released was simple. "I know a few people," Al explained.

Ward didn't know who these friends of Al's were, but from the speed of his release, Ward was sure the police knew them.

"I gave them my word you'd be here tomorrow to make a statement," Al said. "Now, I want you to give me yours."

"You got it."

As they left the police station parking lot in Al's car, Ward took a deep breath of the sweet night air.

"How's B.J.?" he asked.

"That B.J.," Al said with admiration, "she's a real pistol, isn't she? I think it was a good thing for the cops they let you go tonight and didn't have to tangle with her."

"And Nola?"

"Not so good. Doctor says they may have to operate."

Al headed for Painter's Island to pick up the truck, explaining, "I got to go home. Raylene's gonna have a shit fit as it is. You coming back to the Crossroads tonight?"

Ward nodded. "I'm going to the hospital first, and then I'll be along."

"I fed the animals," Al said. "Hadn't noticed before, but that ole wolf's looking pretty seedy. You reckon you ought to take care of him?"

"Yeah," Ward said. "I think so."

The island swarmed with police, but Al had a release form for the pickup. Al shook Ward's hand, said good night and drove off, leaving Ward to retrace the route to Blytheville.

Ward found B.J. sitting alone in a small reception room outside the intensive care unit. Her face was still drawn, but a little color had crept into her cheeks, and her eyes lit with happiness and relief when he walked in.

She told him Nola was still critical. "There's swelling

in the brain. The doctor says we just have to wait and see."

"You ought to get some rest yourself," Ward said.

"I can't leave her. I know it sounds peculiar, but I'm her lifeline right now."

"I need some clean clothes, and there's something back at the zoo I have to take care of," Ward said. "But if you want me to stay—"

"No," she said. "You don't have to. You've done so much already. I don't see how I could ever thank you."

"Then don't. Anyway, I think we're even. B.J.? I hope Nola's going to make it, but remember what I said about letting go."

"I will," she said. "See you tomorrow?"

A hell of a simple question, but it seemed to him loaded with portents and promises.

"Yes," he said. "See you then."

After Ward left, B.J. sat alone in the small room. She ached with fatigue, and her arm throbbed. The local the doctor had used to restitch her wound had long since worn off. Maintaining the link with Nola was the worst drain, though. But she dared not let go. Nola had wandered off to some dark and terrible place, and there was only the most tenuous thread holding them together.

Iris and Denny were out in the camper in the hospital parking lot, Iris having refused to spend good money on a motel. B.J. hoped Ward had dropped by to see them so that Denny would stop worrying.

Earlier, around eight o'clock, Eugene Lasker, the Douglas family attorney, arrived, looking grim and somber. He said he had managed to get in touch with Nola's mother, her only family. He seemed to recall Nola had a boyfriend, but he had no idea how to locate the man. He added more pieces of the puzzle for B.J., explaining about Dorothy Douglas's will and Verna's reaction to it.

Money may have been the root of Frank Moser's attack

on Nola, but B.J. remembered his crocodile gaze and shivered.

No, best not to think about Frank now. She curled up in a chair, closed her eyes, and called to Nola over and over again. She was drifting toward sleep—or worse—when she heard the first faint reply.

Annie?

B.J. sat bolt upright, her heart pounding. A few seconds later a nurse hurried into Nola's room, then the doctor came. He reappeared in a little while to say that Nola was awake and asking for B.J.

"She's going to be all right," B.J. said.

"Well, I couldn't say for sure—"

"She is," B.J. said.

"Let's hope so. Five minutes," the doctor warned.

B.J. went in and sat beside the bed, looking down at the woman who had been a stranger twenty-four hours ago and marveling at the bond between them. Would it fade again as it had when they grew up? Such intensity—she thought it might. But she hoped it wouldn't disappear altogether.

She realized something else, sitting there. Except for Denny, she had really had nobody in her life. Now there was Ward—not a sure thing, but a definite option. And a growing closeness to her mother. And Nola . . . so many wonderful possibilities . . .

Nola opened her eyes, a startling blue against her pale face, and smiled.

"Hello, friend," Nola whispered.

Then she closed her eyes and slipped away, but this time it was into normal, healing sleep.

Ward sat next to Lobo's cage in the shadow of the enclosure, listening to the animal's labored breathing. The Crossroads had just closed. Customers were leaving.

"Not long now," Ward said quietly.

The wolf watched him, eyes glowing dully in the darkness.

When Ward arrived at the Crossroads, he had a brief skirmish with Raylene that Al squelched with a firmness that surprised her into silence. But Ward knew she was a woman who hoarded malice and got her way by dripping her vitriol like water on stone. Good thing he was already planning to move on.

Ward wouldn't be going far of course. Back to the hospital tomorrow, then to the police to clear things up, and, after that—well, he might take a short trip to Florida. A visit with his parents was long overdue. Then he thought he'd come back, find B.J. and Denny, and see if those portents and promises had any staying power.

In the parking lot, the big fluorescents blinked out. The Norrises' Mercury drove away. Ward went to get his gun from his pack and came back to the cage. A horned moon had risen. The night was alive with the sound of crickets and frogs. Ebbie bleated from the pasture.

Time to get on with it, hey, Trag?

"Yeah, it's time," Ward said.

He reached inside the cage and gently stroked the wolf's head for a moment before pressing the gun against it. Then he did what he should have done for Remy all those years ago.

He pulled the trigger and set the wolf free.

Printed in the United States
By Bookmasters